The Mightiest Machine
John W. Campbell, Jr.

The Mightiest Machine

John W. Campbell, Jr.

The Mightiest Machine

John W. Campbell, Jr.

INTRODUCTION

John Wood Campbell Jr. (1910-1971) remains one of the towering figures in twentieth-century science fiction, both as a writer and–perhaps more enduringly–as an editor. Born in Newark, New Jersey, he studied physics (at MIT, then Duke University), and early on showed a fascination with scientific ideas, theoretical possibility, and the machinery of space adventure. His early work under his own name tended toward the adventurous, pulp-style "space opera" tradition: fast-paced, large scale, with interplanetary conflict and alien civilizations. At the same time, under his pseudonym **Don A. Stuart**, Campbell experimented with mood, psychological tension, and more subtle speculation.

In terms of influences, Campbell drew on the pulp traditions of the 1920s and early 1930s: the planetary romances, the imaginings of other worlds, the sense of wonder mixed with loose science. But he also had a more formal scientific grounding which distinguished him from many pulp writers: his physics background and interest in contemporary scientific and pseudoscientific ideas informed not only his stories but his editorial judgments. As editor he pushed for intelligent plot construction, believable extrapolation, and plausible technology, helping move the field beyond mere spectacle.

One of Campbell's most famous stories is *Who Goes There?* (1938), published under the Stuart name. It is a tale of Antarctic researchers who discover a crashed alien ship inhabited by a terrifying, shapeshifting organism. The story is deeply atmospheric rather than sweeping in scale; it explores paranoia, identity, and the unknown. It has been adapted multiple times for film, most famously John Carpenter's *The Thing* (1982), as well as earlier and later versions.

As editor, Campbell's impact is perhaps even greater. From 1937 until his death in 1971 he helmed the magazine *Astounding Science Fiction* (later *Analog*), and in that role he shaped what many consider the Golden Age of Science Fiction. He discovered or nurtured such writers as Robert A. Heinlein, A.E. van Vogt, Theodore Sturgeon, Isaac Asimov, among others. He was not only selecting stories but shaping what science fiction could be: more rigorous, more speculative, more concerned with ideas as well as adventure.

In literature history, Campbell is often considered a pivot between pulp romance, early speculative adventure, and the more thoughtful "classic" science fiction that emerged mid-century. His own space opera novels—the "Arcot, Morey, Wade" series (e.g. *The Black Star Passes, Islands of Space, Invaders from the Infinite*)—may seem dated in certain respects now, but they exemplify early imaginations of galactic scale, inter-planetary travel, and heroism. They provide a foundation upon which later writers built, refining character, plausibility, pacing, stakes.

For readers enjoying Campbell's approach, several other authors offer similar virtues in their space opera work, though each in a different way. E. E. "Doc" Smith's *Lensman* series remains a high-water mark for grand scale cosmic conflict and spectacular technology. Jack Vance's *The Stars My Destination* or *Tschai* books bring a richer sense of culture, weirdness, and character alongside exploration. More recently, authors like C.J. Cherryh (for political intrigue and alien/contact complexity) and Alastair Reynolds (for hard science scale and operatic sweep) build on what Campbell helped put in motion. Those looking for classic space opera with strong ideas might also enjoy Poul Anderson's *The High Crusade* or Edmond Hamilton's *The Star Kings*.

CHAPTER I

"I SUPPOSE," SAID DON Carlisle with a look of disapproval, "that this, too, is the 'latest and greatest achievement of interplanetary transportation engineers.' They turn out a new latest and greatest about once every six months—as fast as they build new ships in other words."

"You should talk!" Russ Spencer laughed. "One of the features of that ship is the new Carlisle air rectifiers, guaranteed to maintain exactly the right temperature, ion, oxygen, and ozone content as well as humidity control. But, anyway," he went on, turning to his friend, "I wish you could have made this discovery just two years earlier. It was the dream of dad's life to build the first meteor-proof ship in the Spencer Rocketship Yards. You physicists were mighty slow about that. You've done the miracle now—I hope—but I wish you could have done it sooner."

Big Aarn Munro smiled his slow smile. "I wish I could have, Russ. But remember, physics is like a chain—you can't add the last link till all the earlier ones are in place. You don't know, perhaps, how much depends on that one discovery of the magnetic atmosphere. I couldn't have done it two years before, because then the necessary background hadn't been developed. Now, the magnetic atmosphere development of mine will serve as background for other developments. While you engineers have been working on this ship, I have, despite Carlisle's contemptuous references, been trying to prepare for another 'latest and greatest.' "

They had reached now, the base of the huge metal ways that supported the newly completed *Procyon*, the Spencer Rocket Co.'s latest product. Nearly seven hundred feet long, two hundred and fifty in diameter, a huge, squat cylinder, it loomed gigantic. The outer hull of aluberyl gleamed with faint iridescent color in the light of the few great lamps scattered about the huge construction shed.

The hum and rattle of saws and welders was subdued here, all the work was being done inside now, and fleets of heavy freight planes were dropping gently into place on the helicopters, bearing loads of furnishings. Lights glowed in some of the ports now, and six huge, twisting cables snaked off across the littered yards to the main power board. The distant rhythm of the great power plant outside echoed faintly even here.

"She taking off on time, Russ?" asked Aarn, looking up at her.

"She should." The engineer nodded. "Barrett said he was sure of his end. Trial run tomorrow starting at 13:57:30 o'clock. Just to Luna City and back. And let's hope, Aarn, that your idea is right." A note of real earnestness had entered Spencer's voice now. "Aside from the fact that she means nearly ten million credits investment, which no one will insure on this trip, there will necessarily be seventy-three men aboard. And I'm taking your word for it and testing her in the worst of the Leonids."

Aarn nodded silently. Then he spoke again: "Physics says they will be safe from anything short of a ton. And meteors weighing even a hundred pounds are mighty rare."

"But it takes only one," Spencer reminded him, "and that one would mean near ruin to me. My grandfather and my father have built up this business. I've had mighty little to do with it—only the last two years since dad died—but I don't want to see the tradition die. My grandfather built the first rocket to reach the Moon back in 1983. Dad built the first rocket to reach Mars back in 2036. Your father rode the first rocket to reach the surface of Jupiter. And mine built it. But naturally the old Spencer rocket had plenty of competition. The *Deutsche Rakete* people being the worst—or best. They'll be on my neck if I lose this. But the little ships worked and, despite what they say about the big field not holding, I'm trusting your figures."

"I'm going along," Aarn smiled. "I'll bet my neck on it, anyway. Physics is generally a pretty safe bet."

"Uhmm—maybe so," Carlisle put in. "But you physicists have done a poor job on the subject of the atom. You've been promising us atomic energy and transmutation for a century, and you can't even tell why a chemical combination takes place."

"I hear," said Aarn slowly, "that you chemists have a theory that will account for it. And that theory also says that tungsten, in an X-ray tube, should radiate in the 'pale pink,' as Morgenthal expressed it."

"Well—that's as good as your physics atoms will do. You predict, similarly, that carbon will combine only with electro-negative elements. And X-rays in the 'pale pink' are no worse than denying the very useful hydrocarbons. And we chemists have produced rocket fuels for terrestrial rockets, while you physicists haven't yet produced atomic energy for interplanetary rockets. Oh, you have a sort of bad compromise in the accumulator—"

"The accumulator is a very useful and compact device," Aarn interrupted, "which holds no less than thirty thousand kilowatt hours per pound—just a wee bit better than you chemists have ever hoped to do. I well remember that we Jovians waited twenty-two long years for release. Chemists made fuels eventually, that would lift a ship from Earth to Phobos—Mars to Jupiter, but couldn't even begin to lift it back. So a few spirits like dad and mother and the rest of the people there just marooned themselves and waited twenty-two years till physics rescued them. Chemistry got them in, but couldn't get them out again."

"Yes; but chemistry made their synthetic foods for them meanwhile."

"Foul things," said Aarn with a grimace. "I was nineteen before I tasted food."

"They seemed to agree with you," said Spencer with a slight smile.

Aarn Munro stood some five feet seven in height, and, to those who did not know him and his remarkable history, appeared exceedingly fat. He was nearly five feet in circumference, while his arms and legs stuck out at peculiar angles. And they seemed misshapen.

Jupiter, a world of two and a half times the gravity of Earth, required strength in its people, and speed, too. On Earth, Aarn weighed nearly three hundred and fifty pounds. For the first twenty years of his life he had lived on the giant of the system, and had developed such strength as no Terrestrian ever dreamed of. More than once he had proved his ability to lift and walk off with a ton and a half of lead.

"They did, chemically," Aarn acknowledged. "But I wasn't sorry to see a ship come in that could get out again."

"But," said Spencer, "if it wasn't for the nice stepladder of satellites, by the way, even Aarn's vaunted physics couldn't get a ship loose from old Jove's grip."

"That's true," returned Aarn, "but it doesn't enter the question, you see, because the satellites *are* there. Nine of 'em. So it's just a case of Jupiter to Five to Europa to Six to Mars. And what better could you ask?"

"I can ask a lot better," Spencer said, his voice suddenly sharp and annoyed. They had reached the main entrance port of the *Procyon*, but Spencer stopped where he was, damming up a stream of workmen, to talk. "I can ask for antigravity apparatus. If physics is any good, it ought at least to be able to say 'Here's the way to do it, but we can't just yet because of this or that,' and then find out how to overcome those difficulties.

"And I could ask for a machine that could generate power. Power from atoms, perhaps. This thing, this big hulking brute, it's a waste of water that this planet may need some day. Look at Mars—dry as dust. Almost impossible to get rocket water there. If it wasn't for the photo cells that give them power direct from the Sun, and make it possible to cook water out of gypsum, they couldn't live. Some day Earth will need water as badly, and this wasting of thousands of tons of water is a crime and a thousand other things.

"Damn it all, Aarn, why don't you do something? Chemistry is helpless. It's a job for physics, and you know it, and so does Carlisle, for all his bluffing. Why don't you do it, though?

"You've done a miracle already in making that magnetic atmosphere, and I know it. The way it stops meteors and burns them into gas is a miracle; but not enough, we need more."

"We do, Russ, and I know it. That magnetic atmosphere was a by-product. It was a first step on the road, just the metal of which the key is made, purely incidental. I haven't been saying much, but I've been doing some extremely interesting work. And—I'm going to tell you a story.

"I saw a machine. It was the mightiest machine that could ever exist. It was an atomic, better, a material engine. It burned matter to energy. Most of the energy was electrical in nature at one stage of the process, but it was converted to heat and light and other forms of energy. And one of those forms of energy was a curious field of force that could tear great holes in tremendous masses of matter, and there appeared coincidentally with that a force that seemed to hurl masses of matter greater than a dozen worlds like Earth, greater than mighty Jupiter, a million miles into space.

"It was a wonderful, pulsing, rhythmic machine, and operated in a wonderful adjustment more delicate than any machine man ever made. Controlling unimaginable billions of billions of horse power, it remained in perfect balance with a variation in its output of less than one per cent. Controlling forces that could have hurled this planet about like a bit of dust, it remained in perfect equilibrium.

"It was a star. Any star. It was the Sun, the mightiest machine man ever observed. A titanic, inconceivable generator handling the power of three millions of tons of destroyed matter every second—and maintaining equilibrium. The explosion of more than three million tons of matter, really, regulated and controlled. Save that occasionally a great rent appears in its surface that could swallow all the planets of the system, and not be filled, or a tongue of flame a quarter of a million miles high and a million miles wide darts out, apparently lifting billions of tons of matter hundreds of thousands of miles against a gravitational force ten times as intense as Jupiter's—twenty-five times Earth's.

"But—does it?"

Aarn looked intently at Spencer, and slowly an expression of wonder spread over the engineer's face.

"Good—Heaven! Antigravity!"

"I only guess that, Russ. I don't know. But I want to have your help now. I need your influence to have all the spaceliner captains make observations of a particular nature. And I need the observations of the lunar magnetometer and electrometer coordinated with a set of readings taken on Phobos and on Satellite Nine. If you get me those—And I've another idea."

Aarn turned and went on into the *Procyon* thoughtfully. The workmen who had been patiently waiting for the big boss to get out of the way started streaming through again.

CHAPTER II

IN THE SUPER-PATIENT TONE one uses when patience is nigh exhausted, Spencer spoke to the grinning Carlisle: "No. Spelled n-o. It is a syllable of negation, and refers definitely to the fact that that blistering, cockeyed son of an aberrating corkscrew, Aarn, has given me no tiniest bit of information. I gave him all the information he wanted.

"I then asked him for one tiny spark of hope. 'Uhh! That isn't what I hope. That's not so good. Still—maybe—my theory may be wrong, but it may not. No; I don't know, Russ. I'll—' And then the clogged rocket goes wandering off on a triple-focus ellipsoid orbit. I can't find out what he was going to do. He's as noisy as a clam playing hide and seek with his best enemy when he starts thinking. The worst of it is that he won't tell me anything at all."

Don Carlisle grinned again in sympathy. "I heard he was making noises like an oyster, so I came over to see. Whose lab is this, anyway?"

Spencer looked at him reproachfully. "Why bring that up? I pay for it, so naturally I can't get in. Since the *Procyon* rode out to the Moon and back through the Leonid meteor shower without a dent, the whole shipyard has been so crowded with orders I couldn't turn round quickly, and he's grown a head as big as Jupiter itself. Before this gravity stunt he was working on something else. 'Super-permeable space' he calls it. Something to do with that 'magnetic atmosphere' of his."

"What," asked Carlisle, "is a magnetic atmosphere? I asked him once, and he explained something about a field of high permeability that did something or other to meteors so that they were electrified and so the field of special permeability became impermeable, and the magnet makes the meteors stop and blow up, because they are iron. Now I, in my simple, childish mind, always thought a magnet attracted iron. It seems I was wrong."

Spencer grinned and answered: "It does. Up to a point, that is. What Aarn did was to discover a way of making lines of magnetic force do something—that gives us an isolated north or an isolated south magnetic pole. Also an electric charge. Aarn says that the magnetic lines of force that represent the other pole are turned through ninety degrees in space and become lines of electric force.

"Anyway, he has a single pole magnet, and that proceeds to surround itself with a uniform magnetic field. It does attract iron and nickel and cobalt, of course, but when the metals fall through the magnetic field they have to cut the lines of magnetic force. In doing so they act as electric generators. Electricity is generated in them and heats them. But heat represents energy, and the heat they generate is generated at the expense of their motion.

"The magnetic field is so intense, and their velocity so great at first, that they are heated almost instantaneously to thousands of degrees centigrade and explode into vapor. As vapor they are not dangerous, and nothing larger can get through. Except, of course, the huge things that are too big for the field to handle, but a meteor weighing five hundred pounds is almost as rare as a comet.

"In other words, this magnetic field serves for the space ship just as the Earth's atmosphere does for the planet. It slows the biggest, and stops and utterly destroys the little ones. It is extremely seldom that a meteor gets through our atmosphere. The magnetic atmosphere is almost equally effective."

"But why will a plain piece of metal, without windings or anything, generate current?" Carlisle objected.

"Say, Car, use your head. That's something you do know—eddy currents—why on that basis, why does a generator generate? Each wire is just a simple piece of metal. You've used the same principle a thousand times. Each electric power meter uses the thing in the control damper disk, the aluminum disk that rotates between the poles of a pair of permanent magnets. Anyway, that's not the important part. The big thing is that Aarn succeeded in making the lines of force lie down around the ship like a sheath instead of standing out like hairs on a frightened cat. It—"

"Hello, boss!" said a deep voice immediately above and behind his left ear. "Won't you come in?"

Spencer rose six inches from his chair in a spasmodic jump and turned on Aarn with a sour face. "You misplaced decimal point, if it weren't for my memories and loyalty to dear old Mass Tech, I'd amputate you from the pay roll."

"Would you?" asked Aarn, with a pensive air. When pensive, Aarn's broad face and huge body succeeded in looking like a cow of subnormal intelligence, ruminating on the possible source of its next meal. He did now. "I'd hate that, Russ. But I think you'd hate it worst. I got my super-permeable space condition. That's about the poorest name imaginable, so I've decided to invent a name. Be it hereinafter referred to by the party of the first part as the 'transpon' condition. Anyway, come on in."

Aarn's workship was large and divided into two parts, the apparatus room, inhabited by four technical assistants who made up the apparatus Aarn called for, and Munro's own sanctum.

In Aarn's inner lab were a series of benches and cabinets and tables. These were all loaded with junked apparatus, unused parts, spare voltmeters, and coils of wire. The floor was reserved for the heavier junk that would have crushed the tables.

Spencer was quite surprised to see that one of the largest benches had actually been entirely cleared, and two sets of apparatus set up on it. Aarn smiled his blank grin again. Spencer knew from sad experience that that smile meant something completely revolutionary that would upset all his calculations and probably cost him, temporarily at least, several million dollars.

"Look," said Aarn.

He waved his hands toward the new apparatus he had set up on the bench. The apparatus consisted of two main groups. At one end of the bench was a squat control panel, backed by a complex assortment of tubes and a device that closely resembled the magnetic atmosphere apparatus connected with a curious wire cone. There was a standard a foot tall surmounted by a cone of copper bars running lengthwise to form the sides and around, binding the longitudinal bars in position.

The tip of the cone was a block of copper, the size of a golf ball. The mouth of the device was some four inches across and the length over all about ten inches. But the copper bars that formed the sides of the cone were carefully insulated from the block that was at the tip. From this block, a single straight bar of copper projected along the axis of the cone.

Aarn smiled and turned on the apparatus. A low, musical hum rose from the tubes and coils, and slowly a faint blue glow centered about the copper block at the tip of the cone and the pencil of metal that extended up the axis. For five seconds this held steady while a similar blue glow began to build up about the outer system of copper conductors. Presently, as this reached a maximum, the inner glow began to fade, then swiftly a pulsing rhythm was set up, first the inner, then the outer conductor system glowing more intensely. The light settled down to a steady flickering that the eye could barely perceive, and Aarn smiled at it thoughtfully.

"The apparatus takes a few minutes to warm up. That's the first half. That was the hardest part, too, curiously, though this projector here is a far more important discovery."

Aarn pushed a second standard into view, which was surmounted by a metal bowl that closely resembled a deep soup dish. The inner surface was evidently a parabolic one, made up of a maze of tiny coils, each oriented carefully toward some definite aim, while the entire rim of the "soup dish" was a single larger coil.

Carefully Aarn adjusted it so that it pointed toward the flickering cage of copper wires, and beyond it to the apparatus at the other end of the bench. This apparatus seemed fairly simple, merely a number of standards with various arrangements of wires. Two parallel copper bars, a double spiral made of two insulated wires, two metal disks.

"Those," said Aarn softly, "are simply connected with the normal power supply. It is alternating current of sixty cycles at two hundred and twenty volts. The device I have is a pick-up. It will collect the power from those wires. The projector here is the real secret—it makes space itself become a perfect conductor of electric-space-strain. Not electricity. Electric-space-strain. But the result is the same. It makes the space along its axis capable of carrying power along the axis—and along the axis only. When I start this, the space between here and that interrupter coil back there will become a perfect conductor. The interrupter coil is necessary to prevent the thing reaching on, out indefinitely.

"The pick-up there, will be in that path of conduction, and so will the first of those lead-offs there. That pair of straight wires. The wires will not be mutually short circuited because this will conduct current only *along* the axis. But the pick-up there keeps sending out flashes of a somewhat similar energy at an angle so that it covers the entire column, and so can pick up the power in it.

"I can't make that pick-up work continuously, because the energies would then interfere and simply short-circuit things. But I can make it work at any frequency from one cycle a second to about fifty megacycles. Now I'm going to adjust it to sixty cycles, and it will get in step with the power on the two leads—and run that series of lights and that motor."

Aarn pushed a switch. Instantly three tumblers snapped over automatically, a powerful surge of power seemed to draw at the men themselves momentarily, and then the little flickering pick-up was sending out searchlight beams of brilliant ionization. They started out along the shape of the cone, spread rapidly, till they filled the tight, round column of power coming from the transpon condition projector, then the ionization stretched along like a luminous liquid flower in a pipe.

"The thing isn't in phase—wasting a lot of power," said Aarn.

He began adjusting a dial, and the slight visible flickering vanished as the frequency rose. Suddenly the ionization all but vanished, leaving only a slight glow about the pick-up itself. Then an instant later it was back, but vanished again. Each time the ionization stopped, the lights glowed, and the motor Aarn had pointed out hummed into speed.

Presently he had it exactly adjusted, and the lights burned steadily, the five horse-power motor continuing smoothly.

"The efficiency is about seventy-five per cent, which is not very good, I'll admit—but good enough for what I have in mind."

Spencer was looking at the device intently. At last he asked: "But why doesn't the pick-up short-circuit the thing when it has thrown out its pick-up force? It throws a conducting band or disk completely across the tube of the transpon beam, as you said you called it. That will carry current at right angles to the axis, so it lies completely across the two terminals of the wires."

Aarn smiled grimly. "That, Russ, is why I took nearly nine months to do this. I had to prevent that. The answer is that the lock and the grid don't project the same force. The grid projects a force which will accept only a negative electric force, while the block will accept only positive. Therefore it can't short-circuit."

"Then it rectifies, too? Some little device! It's a thing we've sought for a century, Aarn—power broadcast along a beam."

"No," said Aarn sharply. "That's the point—it isn't broadcast along a beam. A beam reaches out and picks it up. The difference is as great and as vital as the difference between being hit and stopping something going by. If a man's fist connects with the button, your jaw absorbs kinetic energy. He has broadcast it along the beam of his arm.

"But if you reach out and grab hold of a man running by you, you have reached out for and taken hold of a source of kinetic energy and momentum. Right?"

"Hm—hum! Distinct difference. But why does it count here? What difference does it make?"

"Nut—a system of difference. No beam any man ever made could hold an absolute beam—a fixed diameter from here to infinity. Any power beam you make has to carry so much power per square-inch cross section at the point where the power is picked up. Suppose I'm sending power to a ship going to the Moon. On Earth the beam is ten feet across. Fine, the ship has an absorber or pick-up twenty feet in diameter, let's say. When the ship is fifty miles up, the beam and the pick-up are the same size. At one hundred miles the beam is wasting seventy-five per cent of its power because it has to maintain a certain power at the ship, and only twenty-five per cent of the beam is impinging on the target.

"Now—take it the other way. If the ship projects the beam, the earth power station is simply pouring power into a funnel. The energy can go only one way, and no matter how widespread it is at Earth, it has to get out on the pick-up in the beam. It's bound to be infinitely more efficient after you get more than ten miles away."

"Slightly," agreed Spencer with a smile. "So hereafter, ships won't carry accumulators, eh? Just send back a beam and pick up power from Earth. But say—how are they going to be made to pay for it? They could tap any power source or any line on Earth?"

Aarn smiled and replied: "In the first place, they won't get their power from Earth, and in the second place, just suppose you sent back one of the beams to tap any sixty-cycle line on Earth. What would happen? First, you'd have to get in phase with some one of the big power-line networks. Then, bingo, you have everything from one hundred and ten to one hundred and ten thousand and above volts coming smashing along. It would blow you to kingdom come and wreck the apparatus. Might do some damage back on Earth, but I doubt it."

"Not get the power from Earth? Where then? Not from one of the other planets surely, because they have power troubles of their own."

"From the mightiest machine!"

"Good Heaven! The Sun! Do you mean that thing could tap the awful power of the Sun?"

Spencer's face was suddenly pale. He could visualize that beam as though a visible thing reaching from some tiny dust mote out across space to impinge on the Sun, and drink of the power in that million-mile electric furnace, where matter was smashed beyond atoms, ground to radiation.

"The Sun," Aarn nodded. "It's hard to think of all at once. Tapping the mightiest machine—the most inconceivably huge engine in the universe really—for any star would do. Making a star supply your power. A furnace that consumes nearly four million tons of matter a second.

"It's simple really. You need a power stack, of course—a huge supply of power storage to operate your machine when you were not in position to tap the Sun. It would require only a modification of this device—one I have worked out completely—and we could draw a billion billion horse power in direct current at any voltage you wished, up to a maximum of about five hundred million, which would make insulation impossible in any circumstances."

"Then—unlimited power—and I thought—it was just a new power-transmission device. Atomic energy! Man could never build—of course he couldn't make one as big—a sun—two million million million tons of engine—three hundred thousand worlds like this—"

He laughed suddenly. "Car, you wanted to know why physics didn't give you the atomic energy they promised. Here's physics' answer! Atomic energy would be too expensive—require too elaborate a control—so physics taps a sun!"

CHAPTER III

"THAT," SAID AARN QUIETLY, "is one of the things I promised. Now that we have the power I promised, I think I can also promise the antigravity device."

"Antigravity, too! Say, Aarn, there won't be anything left to find after you get through with physics. But can you? How—"

"The Sun gave that secret, too. It is because the terrific forces beneath the surface cut off the gravity that those huge masses of matter can be ejected to form prominences. I was right—and the data that men out in space collected gave me the necessary basis for my problem's solution.

"Look—for a century or more men have known that there were three types of space-strain energy fields. There is the electric-energy field and the magnetic-energy field, which are mutually at right angles to each other. My 'magnetic atmosphere' device simply turns half of the magnetic field through ninety degrees and makes it an electric instead of a magnetic field pole. That was simple.

"But—gravity has no poles. Gravity is fourth dimensional instead of in three dimensions. I found out the answer, thanks to the Sun. Remember, it takes a three-dimensional thing to have two different types of stresses. Take a rubber balloon as an example. The rubber can be dented inward. A strain along the diameter of the sphere. But the rubber becomes stretched on one side and more or less piled up on the other. Those two types of stress are at exactly ninety-degree angles. That represents magnetism and electric field.

"Obviously, if we dent the balloon inward in one place, it will stretch outward somewhere else to make up for it, perhaps all over, but a swelling takes place. That represents the fact that a north pole is always associated with a south pole, somewhere or other. If the fabric is stretched along its surface, it is thinner in one place, but inevitably piles up elsewhere. Where there is a positive pole there is necessarily an accumulation of negative, somewhere.

"But our rather poor illustration doesn't explain just how the ninety-degree twist is possible except generally in that, if the balloon is dented, if the fabric stretches, there is no actual dent outward. Our model is poor, because space is four dimensional.

"But you see that it requires a three-dimensional medium for two stresses at right angles to each other. It requires four for three right-angle forces. And the curious thing about that four-dimensional stress is that it doesn't have polarity necessarily. But there is a reverse condition. In magnetic and electric fields, opposites attract. In gravity likes attract. That is characteristic. Opposites repel.

"I can make the gravity curvature—given energy enough. I can also make the reverse curvature of space. But before I can reverse curvature of space locally, I have to iron out the normally present gravitational curvature. Any space strain is energy. It requires enormous energy."

Aarn got off the bench where he had been sitting, and started clearing away his last demonstration rapidly, setting up a new group of apparatus.

"Suppose we wanted to free a mass of gravity. To flatten out the local gravity, we have to overcome its own gravity. You know the old lines-of-force picture of magnetism, Spence. You can use that lines-of-force idea on any of the three space fields. In the gravitational picture, it works something like this: the attraction of the Earth for a small body, like this lead weight, for instance, is equaled, of course, by the attraction of the small body for the Earth. If you think of it as lines of force, picture the lines about a small piece of iron in the field of a powerful magnet. The magnetic lines of force bend into and pass through the piece of iron.

"Suppose we wanted to wrap a coil of wire around that bit of iron, and make it 'magnetic-weightless,' so to speak. We would have to build up a magnetic force in our coil that opposed the greater magnetic field and bent the magnetic lines of force away. Then really, in demagnetizing our little piece of iron, we are having to overcome the big field in which it is at least locally.

"Ditto with degravitation. We act as though we were merely trying to make the piece of lead we are working with stop attracting, stop being a source of gravitational force, but in order to do that we have to overcome locally Earth's field, the Sun's field, and all the fields of the universe.

"Actually, of course, this is too much work, and for practical work I will overcome only the solar-system fields. But, even so, that represents a lot of energy. The law of conservation of energy demands that I supply energy equivalent to lifting the degravitized body completely free of the fields by distance, lifting it out to infinity in other words. That's equivalent to the kinetic energy it would have at about sixty miles per second."

Aarn paused. He had his apparatus set up—a strangely shaped series of coils surrounded by a pair of heavy metal plates. A hollow space of about a thousand cubic inches remained in them, and in this space now, Aarn was arranging a lead sphere suspended from one arm of a long-arm balance. It was balanced at the other end by a group of weights totaling five pounds.

From the coils, two heavy copper cables ran, twisted, off to the main power board on the other side of the room. His apparatus ready, Aarn walked over to the panel and laid his hand on the main power control.

"Ready, I guess. Keep an eye on that lead, Spence, and see if you can keep it balanced!"

Aarn flipped a small switch, a relay thunked over, then rapidly he advanced his controller. For perhaps ten seconds nothing happened.

"Induction—she's building up a magnetic field in there now, and an electric pole, too," Aarn explained.

Then—abruptly, yet leisurely, the weight pan of the long-arm balance sank.

"The weight's going!" called Spence excitedly.

"It should!" Aarn grinned. "She's drawing two thousand horse power."

Carlisle watched interestedly as Spencer took weight after weight from the balance pan. Still the scale remained steady. "It's two and a half pounds now—"

"That's about enough," decided Aarn. "I just wanted to show you."

"Can you make Earth's centrifugal force throw it up?"

"I could—in about four and a half years with this power source. That thing begins building up a back force that makes it hard to pump in juice. That's not the latest design—I've found ways to improve the thing since that was made, which will all be incorporated in the real apparatus. Further, remember, while that's going down fairly fast now, destroying weight is like filling a fuel tank. You can fill a vacuum a lot easier and faster than you can a fuel tank with two tons per square inch in there already. It will begin to show up pretty quickly now. When the weight gets down to about five hundredths of a pound, it will go very slowly."

Aarn reached over, and made some adjustments on his power board, and all but two meters dropped to zero.

"I'm just holding that now. There's no need to de-weight it, is there? We can't do anything real till we have a big job, and a Sun-tapping beam to run it. It builds up an electric-field back-force of several thousand volts; that's what was stopping that then. With the Sunbeam and a big model I can demonstrate. And—uh—well, I have something else, too. But I'm not ready yet," Aarn hastened to add.

Spencer had started up expectantly when Aarn said he had even more. Now he looked at him disgustedly. "As I told Carlisle, you're as noisy as a clam in hiding when you've got something interesting to puzzle about. Now let me ask a question: How do you know that Sun beam will work? Have you tested it on old Sol?"

Aarn smiled faintly and waved him away. "This isn't my home planet—but even so I like it. I said that got power from the Sun. The ionizing layer, my lad, conducts. Could you imagine what would happen if you short-circuited the Sun? That's why the ship we're going to build as a testing laboratory—we'll need a space laboratory now, and it'll cost you five millions, Spence, my boy—will have a huge bank of these new storage devices.

"You know how much energy accumulators will store. These gravitational coils will store electric power at high voltage and about one thousand times the capacity per pound. We need the storage for the times when you are in an atmosphere, behind a planet, or similarly hindered. Here's a point to remember—you can't have those Sunbeam ships wandering about aimlessly. They'll have to be very strictly limited. One of those fellows could cut a swath through any other ship."

"Whew—what a weapon!" gasped Spencer as he pictured it. "Cut a world in two with that and the Sun's power."

"Uhm—deadly enough if you could get in position, but that beam is tender in its way. If you just remember these two facts, you'll see why it really isn't much of a weapon, and isn't to be greatly feared on the score of blowing up a world. That it could be dangerous to a certain extent, is of course true. But remember, that world will have the first chance to put power on the beam. Suppose you are waiting for that beam, and the instant it hits your world you unload a few million volts and a hundred thousand ampere-hours of accumulators on it as just the frequency it's turned for? Good-by, projector.

"Or suppose you had your beam already developed, reaching from ship to Sun, it would take about a quarter of an hour to develop a beam from the Earth to the Sun because of the finite speed of light—and just wait for the world to move into it. You have to send a signal down the beam which determined to what extent you are going to tap the Sun, naturally, or the Sun would just send a flood that would wipe you out before you could shut it off.

"Then if you signaled for unlimited power, so that you could really damage a world, you'd be wiped out first. And always you have to wait the quarter of an hour or so for the energy to make a round trip—and if it's war, somebody will be out looking for you with something bigger than a mosquito spray."

"I shouldn't have cared to develop it if it had been as dangerous as it might have been," Spencer said quietly. "But then, why did you say you couldn't use it in an atmosphere?"

"Short-circuiting the beam is the signal for unlimited power. Hold it on long enough, and you'd get the power."

"Right enough, and tell me why I have to build that five-million-credit flying laboratory," demanded Spencer.

"So I can test out a few things. And—uh—don't put any rockets in it. Get out of the lab here and let me work."

Wherewith Aarn reached out two great arms like tree trunks, and lifted Spencer in one hand and Carlisle in the other, deposited them outside his door, and locked it.

Carlisle looked at the door sourly and brushed himself. "He didn't have to do that to me. I wasn't so damn interested I had to be thrown out."

"Oh," said Spencer hopelessly, "that guy's got my psychology down to a hair line. He knows I won't be happy till I know why we won't need rockets. How in the name of the Nine Wandering Worlds is he going to drive a ship in space without rockets? I can accept his antigravity, because we've known that was coming for a century.

"His Sun beam as he calls it—that's as breath-taking, as utterly original and brilliant as anything man ever did. The colossal, unmitigated gall of a man that will light his cigarette from the fires of the Sun! It would take a man without nerves, without fear, to think of anything as utterly outrageously and gloriously bold as to tap the mightiest machine, as he well called it, for power.

"But now that he's done it, anyone can see that that's the obvious source of power.

"But what's the next stunt?" He, too, looked at the door with anguish.

The door opened abruptly, and Aarn's head appeared. "And, Carlisle, I'll further demonstrate that physics' theories of the atom have their uses."

The head disappeared.

A slow smile spread over Carlisle's face as he looked at Russ Spencer. "I'll bet that information was just enough to give you a complete headache," he said gravely.

CHAPTER IV

"CAR," SAID SPENCER WITH bitterness, "it's a pleasure to call you in here. It's a great soothing agent to have someone pay some attention to you when you ask him to come. For the past week I've been asking Aarn to take an hour off and come have a conference on the ship. The framework plans he sent have been converted into steel and aluberyl. The plates have been welded on. The thing is now a completed hull. But Aarn won't come."

"Has a name been picked for it?" asked Carlisle unsympathetically. "If not, may I suggest *Little Sunbeam*?"

Spencer looked even more aggrieved. "Little credit-eater would be more appropriate. It has cost me two and a half million so far."

"What? Two and a half million? How come, if it's just a hull?"

"Oh, he had a lot of machinery made for it—lot of stuff all ready to install, but he hasn't had time to get around to—"

"Great spaces and little meteors! What was that?"

The entire office building was still trembling and shaking to the sudden strain. It had been a violent howl of terrible wind, an abrupt clutch as of starting space ship's acceleration, a wrench and quiver that shook the very ground and rock beneath them. In the instant that straining yank endured, the wind became a live, shuddering, whining thing that whimpered in terror and rushed into some unknown thing.

The telephonescope clucked and buzzed suddenly. Spencer reached over and flipped his end on, and instantly Aarn's face appeared.

Russ beat him to the draw: "What," he demanded, "in the name of the Nine Wandering Worlds did you do that time?"

Aarn smiled slowly and answered: "Miscalculated. The range wasn't controlled right. It is now. Want another one?" He disappeared for an instant, and during that instant the yank and strain and howling wind reappeared. "I have," announced Aarn slowly, "proved a further use of physical atomic theory. And I will come over. How far is it from where I am to your office?"

"Seven and a half miles," answered Spencer blankly.

Aarn disappeared from view; the telephonescope went blank. For some seconds Spence continued looking on the screen.

"But why do you want to know that, you knew it already?" he asked inanely of the blank screen.

"Open the window for him, will you, Spence. I'm lazy."

———◆———

Carlisle waved a negligent hand toward the office window, a wide sheet of crystal-clear glass that opened on a pleasant rolling mountainside, for Spencer's office was in one of his own buildings. Just now the view was obscured by Aarn's ponderous figure. He was apparently lying on a metal beam about an eighth of an inch thick, and six feet long by ten inches wide, floating in the air. At the forward end of it was mounted a torpedo-head shaped object which evidently acted as combined air break, engine room, and control panel.

For at least forty-five long seconds Spencer stared blankly at the figure calmly lying there. Then Aarn's annoyed voice came through the window: "The walrus is getting a bit tired of being stared at. Open the window and let me in."

Spencer opened the window with a jump and dodged out of the way as Aarn's strange device suddenly spun on an axis about the engine head, and darted straight through the window at a speed of fully seventy miles an hour, and instantly stopped dead in the center of the room.

"This," said Aarn calmly, settling himself as though on a couch in the middle of the room and resting on air, "represents a model of our ship laboratory. You noticed the speed I made coming over. It is seven and a half miles. I came at a speed of nearly one thousand miles an hour, because this device can accelerate and decelerate rather rapidly. I would have been able to get here sooner, you see, if I had had better control. But I have had this thing in working order only about six hours."

"But what is it, you asteroid? What is it?" demanded Spencer, trying to get near it, but it moved away with delicate precision each time he approached.

"A model of our ship lab. It has antigravity, of course. Improved, I may say. I can't dismount here, and every time you try to enter my de-gravitational field the thing shies away, because you have weight.

"That is not new. But the little device I use in driving it is new. Now look here."

Aarn raised the metal hood of the torpedo-shaped head, and displayed the several pieces of apparatus contained therein.

"That is the antigravity device. It is charged with nearly fifteen thousand credits' worth of your power. This is the storage apparatus. It stores up the power I need for running the thing in a type of gravity field. Remember that a gravity field represents an energy storage also, but more intense storage is possible than in magnetic or electric. In this little thing is about three thousand credits' worth of power.

"The third and fourth devices—here and here—are really interconnected and balanced to work as one piece. They are the momentum and kinetic energy devices. Both momentum and kinetic energy involve time, remember.

"But the important thing comes from the wave-mechanics consideration of matter and energy. Remember that an electron is like a photon—it behaves both as corpuscle and as wave in various conditions. Wave mechanics explain that something like this: the electron is always a wave, but can behave like a corpuscle because the waves which make up the true electron and extend through all space—to infinity and back—interact and pile up in one place to make a noticeable knot of energy we call an electron. In only that one limited place do the waves pile up and add to each other. Everywhere else in all infinity the waves are so arranged as to cancel out, but they are there just the same.

"That is one phase of the wave-mechanics atom. And it is the phase that so annoys Carlisle here. He can't make his waves react and produce sulphuric acid.

"Seriously, I agree that is an objection. But, you see, one of the things a consideration of wave mechanics produces is very interesting. It is really two things—two formulas. One shows that momentum is something of the nature of a wave formation. The other shows that velocity also is a wave formula.

"In other words, if we produce the right waves, we would have momentum synthetically produced, and the same for velocity. That means momentum and velocity can be 'tuned in,' and we have that long-sought thing—a driving device that reacts on space itself. Not the empty space you see outside the portholes of a rocket. The physical space of gravitational fields and dynamic strains, of tremendous moving fields of force that tug and weave and pull. Space isn't empty. It's alive with a billion billion strains and stresses. They are physical and real and solid.

"And there are the infinitely extending canceled waves of every electron and every proton in space. That space is solid, firm, something whose fabric is tougher than any metal ever could be. That's the space this device works on.

"It's an oscillator that sets up an oscillating field of force about itself that extends for some ten feet in all directions at full power, lesser distance at lower power, and somewhat modified by the presence of matter within it. It is an oscillation between magnetic, electric, and gravitational fields of force, a circular motion through those three of perfectly inconceivable frequency. I don't quite get it myself.

"Only I can control it. Doesn't take the amount of energy you'd expect because, remember, it isn't like the blessed rocket which has no relativity. This has. It takes about ten times the energy you'd expect for high speeds, and actually produces energy at lower speeds. I can measure an 'absolute' speed with this. I can determine the velocity of the universe—or this part of it, at least—relative to Earth.

"This catches its fingers in the web of space, and I can either drag on it, or push on it, but it does have that relative base, whereas the rocket, with no relative base to work against, of course, apparently violates all laws of physics—at least two of them."

"But how about the velocities we use in interplanetary work?" demanded Spencer.

"Comes under head of low velocities. Doesn't matter, anyway, because you can tap the Sun for power. But it is providential that we don't have to obey the laws of physics when we use rockets. Otherwise we'd never have gotten anywhere.

"Now for a ship the size of the one we will have—about five thousand tons, I calculated—since we are eliminating the heavy double hull, and most of the weight of the outer one, with the magnetic atmosphere—that will be helped any time we have an antigravity field, because the antigravity—I call it an 'aggie' field, by the way—tends to bounce anything coming toward it. The incoming gravitational field, which is what the meteor represents, is repelled by the aggie field.

"To go on; a large weight will be added, however, in the power stacks. We'll carry nearly a thousand tons cargo of power apparatus. With that we can give a jolt that would smash a small planet."

"It would," agreed Spencer, "but inasmuch as it would also smash a large bank roll, tell me, pray, why your soul cries out for such luxuries. What's all that power for?"

"Intense fields; there are peculiar effects when the fields become intense. I might find the secret of the destruction of matter if I could get a sufficiently intense field. Remember, while this Sun-tapper beam is wonderfully better than a rocket, it's a darned inconvenient form of power supply."

"It would take you a year to charge the fool thing," objected Spencer, "even with the Sun beam. You couldn't carry that along your copper bus-bars fast enough."

"Quite true! That's why we'll use power beams. That and the fact that I want to see what power I can send through one of these accelerators. You know the beauty of this form of drive is that there is no feeling of acceleration, since, naturally, all the particles of matter are accelerated individually. You'll be quite weightless in this thing—except for artificial gravity."

"In the meantime, I'm at last ready to discuss this ship thoroughly," acceded Aarn with a smile.

"Uh—you are? Well, I'm ready to discuss that new device. I've got a ship on the ways; it's going to be the *Daniel Spencer* and carry one thousand passengers. The present idea was to have it equipped with magnetic atmosphere, your so-called aggie field, and Sunbeam apparatus. By the way, that gave me a headache—trying to figure out a way to keep the beams pointed at the Sun, and yet not be able to cut across the ship accidentally on a sudden turn. A complicated mess of gyroscopes that's worse than the automatic navigational control, but it will do the job. And now this new stuff has to go on her right away."

"Her? I thought you said it was the *Daniel Spencer*!" Aarn said mildly. "At any rate, I'll have to give you data for it. There's plenty of work on the calc before you can begin. The installation depends on the mass, distribution of mass, and so forth. Now look—"

Carlisle listened patiently for half an hour, then fell into a peaceful, resting sleep.

CHAPTER V

THE OFFICIAL TITLE OF the craft was to be "Spencer Laboratories No. 6." Being human, Aarn wanted to make it capable of a lot more than merely plugging around in space and experimenting. He loaded the design with plenty of aggie power storage coils, and he made the momentum-wave drive apparatus a lot more powerful than was really necessary. The antigravity apparatus was designed to be able to lift the mass of the ship laboratory away from the very surface of the Sun, against a gravitational acceleration of thirty earth-gravities.

All in all, Aarn made that ship an extremely powerful machine. But then—she was designed for experiments.

She was three months building on the Spencer ways. They rushed her construction, too, for many of the devices that Aarn planned to incorporate in later designs needed testing in actual operation. Her hull of beryl-steel was finished within two months, but the new labor of installing the strange devices took time and experimentation, careful, accurate balancing, lest failure be due not so much to defect in plan, as defect in execution.

The final test, her maiden flight in space, Aarn wanted to make alone. "I can operate this thing alone, just as well as I can with a crowd along. I'll let Canning here go—I might need one technical assistant."

"The air apparatus might break down," suggested Carlisle, grinning. "You'll have to take me to be safe."

"The financial apparatus has nearly broken down already, so you'll have to take me. I need a rest." Spencer groaned. "They say I'd be bankrupt now if it weren't that I've got so many orders coming in we can't fill 'em. Man, you may be good in physics, but you don't know how good you are at spending money. I've spent three or four fortunes having dies cut for the apparatus in this boat. This is my little ray of light and hope—if it doesn't come back, I never want to know it. I'm going along."

"Maybe some pirates will hold you up for ransom," suggested Carlisle cheeringly.

"Speaking of your little ray of light and hope and pirates makes me think. This thing needs a name—not a designation, a name. This is our little *Sunbeam*—and may she raise some blisters. She would, by the way, if she hit something going at her maximum," suggested Aarn.

"And if you insist on the whole neighborhood coming, bring Martin, anyway. I want some more meals. If you really want to know why I wanted to go alone, I wanted to go back to Jupiter. For once in my life I could go home without almost having to buy the ship that took me there.

"If you are so insistent, come along, and we'll make it a party."

Three days later, the *Sunbeam*, with five aboard her, took off gently. Up through the great ceiling of the Spencer plant, she angled slowly. She was rising on pure lack of weight, by centrifugal throw. Presently a Spencer salvage ship came over, dropped a huge tow-magnet on the ship, and both rose swiftly into the air. Aarn was afraid to try out the new drive on so powerful a ship when near a planet.

Her crew on that trip that was to lead them to infinity and beyond consisted of Aarn Munro, Carlisle, Spencer, Canning, Aarn's chief technical assistant, and Henry Martin, chief cook and bottlewasher for the expedition.

The tow ship carried her out of the atmosphere and then fell well behind. Gently Aarn stirred in his seat. "And now comes the test. Do we move too slow or so fast we can't handle it? I'd hate to have to charge and rebalance these circuits. Anyway—"

Gingerly he advanced the acceleration control. Softly, behind them the great transpon beams began to hum. Inaudible, invisible, almost indetectable momentum waves began to bite deep into space and thrust the great mass of the ship forward.

The control at one, the *Sunbeam* moved off under one earth-gravity acceleration. Aarn moved his control to two. A frown came across his face, then a soft whistle of surprise. His accelerometer had moved over to eight!

"Sweet spirits of space! I was over-conservative. I thought I might not have that figured quite right—and I didn't. I'll have to cube every one of these readings here—and the top one is one thousand!"

"A million gravities! We can't stand that, can we?"

"Well, if the ship can deliver it as a momentum wave, we can stand it. Right now I'm going to take a little run down to old Sol and charge up."

Aarn turned the *Sunbeam* till the electric-blue flame of the heart of the solar system flared in the forward control window. Slowly Aarn advanced his control. At first no visible change occurred, save that Earth fell away; then it was lost from view as it came almost directly behind. Only the one-hundred-million-mile-distant Sun remained visible. Then, slowly, even it began to change; more and more swiftly it expanded till Spencer sat gripping the arm rests fiercely. The tremendous distance to the Sun was being cut down visibly.

"Fifteen hundred miles per second," said Aarn comfortably, "and rising smoothly. Heaven help the meteor we hit. I've got the magnetic atmosphere at full force and tied it in with the whole aggie-coil system. If we hit anything now, it'll get hit first by the magnetic atmosphere, then the antigravity field, and finally the whole impact of our momentum-wave system. We've got the momentum of a major planet packed into a space one mile in diameter!"

"Yes, but suppose we do hit something—the Sun, at the rate you're going now—and get cooked?" suggested Carlisle uncomfortably.

"I'm slowing." Aarn laughed happily. "Spence, you've got a ship as never was before!"

"Don't I know it? The system record for speed is only one thousand, six hundred and thirty-one miles per sec."

"Was, Spence, was—we're doing about eighteen now. And I'm going to stop her dead!"

Aarn threw over a tiny tumbler—his emergency brake. Instantly a terrible crashing roar thundered out of the power room behind, as the transpon beams suddenly felt the impact of countless billions of horse power. Under an acceleration of one million earth-gravities, the *Sunbeam* came to rest and stopped. Not the slightest sign of strain or stress did the men aboard her feel as their "weight" was suddenly increased to around one hundred thousand tons each.

"The *Sunbeam*," decided Aarn judiciously, "is thirsty. We'll give her a drink at the fountain of power—old Sol!"

The *Sunbeam* had started out with barely one tenth of her maximum charge. This had been brought in laboriously by the smaller ships, the Spencer salvage corps. These ships had been equipped with aggie-coil power racks, and transpon beams. The small coils had been charged, then drained into the greater coils of the *Sunbeam*—a ferry system for power, since the transpon beam to the Sun could not safely be used through the atmosphere.

Now the *Sunbeam* was about to drink deep of solar power. A brief roar of sound from the power room told of the establishment of the powerful fields that were projecting the transpon condition through space at the maximum velocity—one hundred and eighty-six thousand miles per second. The Sun loomed gigantic, unbearable, less than thirty million miles away.

Swiftly the silent minutes passed as the five men waited for the return of the power up the beam. Four—five minutes—then with a terrific roar that dwarfed the former protest as the *Sunbeam* was brought to a dead stop, the power came in.

For ten long minutes the roar continued, before Aarn swiftly cut it down, and as he cut it, the hitherto invisible transpon beam reaching from ship to Sun became visible as the excess energy flared off in waste light and heat. In three minutes more, the *Sunbeam* was fully charged.

"She's charged, and ready to ride!" Aarn sighed. "To Jupiter we go—and I'm going to wind up some speed this time!"

The *Sunbeam* turned, and Jupiter rode into view, five hundred million miles away. To the left, Mars glowed dully red-green. Aarn pushed his controller over slowly. Farther and farther. Then slowly, infinitely slowly, Mars began to expand more and more quickly until it was ballooning swiftly, and with a sudden rush swept by them. They were lifting now, lifting in a great arc out of the planetary orbits, up and over the meteor-infested asteroid belt. Five—ten million miles. A needle on a dial before Aarn was quivering against its stop pin, the last reading, forty thousand, well behind it. The *Sunbeam* was going over fifty thousand miles a second.

"She's rolling!" Aarn grinned. Skillfully he looped gently back into the orbital plane, as he snapped his controller back to zero, reversed a tumbler, and pushed up again for deceleration. "We haven't room in this puny little system for this baby—she needs free space to work right."

———— ◦ ————

Aarn was right. The *Sunbeam* needed free space to work in.

Invisible, a dark, jagged mass of age-old broken planet, riding in one of those ultra-eccentric, unpredictable orbits, was far, far out of the asteroid belt. One hundred tons of solid, tough nickel-steel, the same sort of stuff men had been collecting for a century from space to make armor plate.

Aarn was right when he said the *Sunbeam* had the momentum of a major planet—concentrated. Traveling at about forty-two thousand miles a second, slightly less than a quarter of the speed of light, the *Sunbeam* struck that hundred-thousand-ton mass of metal.

For the millionth part of a second, Aarn caught a glimpse of that jagged mass, suddenly illuminated by the light of the Sun—then the magnetic atmosphere struck it. Driven by the full-fed aggie coils, new charged from the fires of the Sun, the magnetic forces shrieked horribly and ripped the mass to incandescent gas in a hundred thousandth of a second. Then the individual molecules slipped unresisted through the forces—still with a mass of a hundred thousand tons. The gravity field and the momentum waves struck it simultaneously.

Space itself shrieked under the impact. Torn by forces beyond even its endurance, space tore open—the *Sunbeam*, part of the now-gaseous meteor, and the contending forces simply dropped through to where neither force nor mass nor energy had meaning.

In the space liner *Aldebaron* Captain Arnold Barrett wrote in his log book:

"At 13:45:30 o'clock, May 14, 2079, a terrific burst of light appeared about ten million miles away, out of the plane of the orbits, and persisted for about five minutes, gradually dying away. It was a curious ring-shaped light, dark in the center for a moment, then suddenly bright as though with a violet sunlight shining through from beyond, then dark again.

"For some time, not even stars beyond this blackness showed, but gradually they reappeared. The duration of the blackness was accompanied by certain peculiar phenomena described by Chief Engineer Rand.

"Chief Mate Matterson reports definitely that he saw a new-type ship, believed to be the new experimental ship of the Spencer Co., moving toward the point where the phenomena appeared shortly before it happened. Matterson reports also, however, that he could see the ship moving against the background of the stars. The distance must have been over ten millions of miles, so he is probably mistaken. No ship could move visibly at that distance."

CHAPTER VI

A BLAST OF LIGHT that was almost physically painful struck Aarn Munro, and he moved restlessly, then jerked abruptly erect. He was facing the control window, and outside he could see six strange ships, each about two hundred feet long, needle-slim, with a tiny visible control-room port, and a ring of projections studding the nose. And the nose of each pointed toward the *Sunbeam* steadily; only occasionally did one swing and dart suddenly to a new position. Powerful beams of bluish light were sweeping over their ship as they apparently investigated.

"What happened?" asked Spencer tensely, suddenly coming up beside Aarn.

"Struck a big meteor. Don't quite know what happened. Ever see ships like those?"

"No known and recognized shipyard of the system ever turned those out," snapped the designer.

"I didn't think so. Did you notice the stars beyond?"

Spencer looked puzzled at his friend, then out toward space beyond. But it wasn't, he suddenly realized, black space. It was silver. It flamed and glowed and sparkled like a curtain of the magnetic atmosphere. There were stars, great brilliant white-hot suns scattered so thickly that space could scarcely show through. The heat from those myriad suns was almost palpable even here.

"Where are we?"

"Don't know—only know where we aren't," replied Munro, his eyes darting swiftly over his instruments.

The ships outside were circling closer now. They had evidently decided the ship was totally dead.

"We aren't in the solar system. I—I've an idea. It seems rather fantastic—but it would explain it, perhaps. You have to admit we are at least one hundred thousand light-years away from where we started—farther really—because those suns I see out there would make the Milky Way a dim thing.

The Milky Way flung across that bunch would show up as a dark ribbon—literally. Actually, we must be a million light-years away. Or more.

"That's a globular cluster, and it's about one hundred thousand light-years or more in diameter, at the minimum. I've spotted three supergiant, type-O stars. That's hot enough to melt the rivets out of a solar investigator at half a light-year. Those three can't be closer than one hundred thousand light-years.

"Those fellows outside are getting bolder. They'd come in but the magnetic atmosphere has them worried. I see it's still on. The momentum oscillations have broken down. A transpon beam lead gave way. The antigravity field has collapsed, and we're falling freely into the local sun. There is one, though we can't see it just now, and it must be a hot one. Look at the color of the light on those ships. It's violet—positively violet.

"They'll try to crack us soon. Take these controls. I'm going back." Aarn leaped. The artificial-gravity apparatus was still functioning, but an Earth gravity didn't bother Aarn much. He met Carlisle on the way back. Carlisle was looking over the air apparatus, which seemed to have stopped functioning.

"Your transpon lead has failed," snapped Aarn as he passed. "I'm going to set it up in a few seconds."

Martin, Spencer's man, who had been brought along in his capacity of chief cook and bottle washer, was just coming out of his galley, his head in his hands. The acceleration neutralization was not quite perfect down so far from the center of the ship, and when they struck the meteor, he had been somewhat shaken up.

"Martin—come along. And call Bob."

Bob was the assistant electronics engineer whom Spencer had brought along. Bob was actually Dr. Robert Canning, and besides being an electronics engineer, he was a clever and skilled mechanician.

———◆———

Aarn was in the control room. In fifteen seconds he had found the defective lead, cut it out with a pair of bolt clippers, and was disconnecting the studs when Canning showed up with Martin.

"Hey, lazy, get a new number twenty-seven lead. Martin, you get the liquid copper, will you?"

"Sorry—didn't come to right off. Saw the planetoid just before we hit, and passed out. What's the matter?"

Canning was back with the bus bar and snapped it in place. Aarn ran down the studs and painted it with the electro-copper solutions Martin brought, solutions which would make the copper surfaces knit electrically, but not too firmly, physically.

"Plenty—we aren't in the solar system—strange ships—looks like attack."

Aarn was busy with the sun beam controls. He was thinking rapidly, and changing settings slowly, he examined the aggie-coil charges, and found that the banks were still about one third charged. He tested the connecting transpon beams to the momentum apparatus. Something more delicate had given away, also, for there was no response whatsoever.

"Nuisance—isn't it?" said Aarn.

He dived across the ship as though there had been no artificial gravity, then leaped halfway to the control room and took over the controls again with less than two minutes' absence.

"They've been sticking instruments into our field," said Spencer, moving out of Aarn's way. "They probably detected our actions when you changed the aggie-coil power distribution. What's up?"

"Wanted current. No great voltage," replied Aarn. "The momentum apparatus is dead, and Canning's working over it."

"The air's working again," said Carlisle, entering. "I've been looking at the stars. Where are we?"

"Too far away to say. I think, though, and hope, that we are in another four-dimensional space. We've gone from our universe to another one through perhaps a five-dimensional nothingness. Like going from one three-dimensional world to another three-dimensional world through a four-dimensional nothingness.

"That's a high-explosive torpedo of some sort he's sending over. I noticed they stripped the hide off of it."

A long, slim device, perhaps a foot in diameter, and twenty feet long had started out of one of the projections on one of the ships. "High explosive—or I'm a chemist instead of a physicist."

The torpedo drifted swiftly, under air pressure evidently, for about a hundred yards, then abruptly the tail became wreathed in smoke, and the thing hurled itself forward violently. It darted at the *Sunbeam*—and suddenly exploded halfway.

"Hmmm—pardonable mistake. They thought that brass and copper would be unaffected by the magnetic field. Stripped off the iron evidently."

Aarn was busy. He was checking, instrumentally, a dozen circuits. At last he called out: "Canning—test circuit MM 433-a."

"That's it," came back the reply. "Compensator broke down. The damping effect when the meteor struck was too great for it. Needs a whole new circuit. Take me at least four hours. Shall I start right now?"

"Well, if you can think of some other way of making this bathtub move, all right, but I thought fixing it might be best," suggested Aarn gently. "What else might we do? Get going."

Aarn was busy with something else. He had the television device working now and was rapidly fitting the heavy mirror-polish steel shutters over the ports of the control room.

"Martin—hey, Martin! Get busy slapping on the port shutters. Fast!"

"Why? Rays do you think?" Carlisle asked anxiously. "We have no defense at all."

"Yes—rays of a sort—light rays; nothing much more dangerous. But light rays could blind us. Remember that the televisor eye there is a photo-cell of the newest Dinwiddie type. They can handle the Sun's radiation at the surface, fifty horse power per square inch. Also, curiously, they are supersensitive. Result—we have an eye out there now that can stand anything any projectors they have can handle."

"Suppose it's a heat ray?" suggested Carlisle.

"Suppose it's your grandmother's pet boogey! Get this through your head, Carlisle: Any weapon that depends on pure energy to destroy is a double-ended weapon, as deadly at the sending end as at the receiving, and probably more so. In other words, to project a heat ray requires the projection of, at least, ten thousand horse power in a beam of not more than half a square foot of cross section. That's not going to be any too bad. But if it's half a square foot at the receiving end, it can't be larger at the sending end, and will probably be smaller. Then it is bound to be more deadly to the projector than to the receiving surface.

"Same's true of anything of the sort. Bombs are like that. They blow themselves—Ah—here he comes."

A ray of light. It was a terrific, stabbing searchlight intended for the sole purpose of blinding the enemy, if it was humanly possible. It would have been effective but for the fact that the televisor simply arranged itself for the necessary load, and showed each ship as a single point of bluish light, not too bright. Then a series of splashes of reddish light began to spread over the surface of the magnetic atmosphere.

"I only fear we are like the oyster and the starfish." Aarn sighed. "They can't break our shell at the present rate, but, on the other hand, we can't run away for a while. But if they just go right on pulling long enough, they may open us up eventually."

The pyrotechnic display stopped abruptly, the searchlights went black, and the television screen showed again the simple ships, their tiny noses an almost impossible target for any weapon.

"Those," said Aarn at length, "are what the old navies would have called destroyers. Speedy probably, fairly powerful fighting weapons, and a very small target."

"What are they going to do next?"

"How in blazes do I know? I guessed the searchlights because it's obvious. The next may be anything from a radio-frequency pencil of energy designed to heat us generally—that being a possibility because, Carlisle, it starts out as electric forces, and doesn't become destructive, unmanageable heat till it's absorbed, but it can't be used as a concentrated beam for cutting holes, because it won't focus that sharply. Or their next attack may be some kind of a tractor beam with which to tow us home where the big battleships can be turned loose on us, to crack the nut; or open the oyster, as I said before."

"What do we do in that case?"

"We help Canning with his repairs as much as possible. And at the end of about four hours, we run away from the bad boys. By the way, we're turning slowly, and we get a peek at the sun in a few minutes. I didn't look when I was back."

"Hmmm—our friends evidently chose the tractor beam. In this case a series of powerful electromagnets on the ends of cables."

The enemy ships were lowering something cylindrical, and roughly fashioned, at the end of long cables toward them. The devices came from somewhere behind, for the cables hung along the side of the ships.

Aarn smiled. "My brethren, we shall now demonstrate the old Australian custom, or 'How to Make a Boomerang Go Home and Spank Papa.' They went to the trouble of making those bar electromagnets to act on our unipolar field. Nice of them—"

Aarn was adjusting something, and he had a switch—a two-way switch—under his hand. The bar magnets the enemy were lowering were taut on their cables now, straining at the powerful unipolar field of the *Sunbeam*.

And with a gentle sigh, Aarn reversed the *Sunbeam's* magnetic pole. Instantly, the half-ton magnets were under the influence of a tremendous magnetic field of the same sign—and they were repelled with all the power that had attracted them, plus a little extra Aarn had added to the field.

Straight and true the great lumps of steel shot backward and toward the needle ships. Two ships avoided their flying magnets, four were struck and dented, one actually torn by the great flying projectile.

"How sweet the uses of adversary!" misquoted Aarn. "But they won't assume we are dead any longer. The fact of life has been adequately proved."

Whoever "they" may have been, "they" didn't. The six ships spun with startling speed into a hemisphere, all ships pointing toward the *Sunbeam*, but so arranged as to offer the absolute minimum target, and the absolute optimum of effectiveness. Then they began running through their armory vigorously.

They started with shells. And they weren't all metal shells this time; a lot of them were evidently made of synthetic plastics and they shot through the magnetic atmosphere unhindered, but now Aarn had re-established an antigravity field, and the great shells bounced one after another into flaming destruction.

⊸◦⊶

The terrific searchlights flamed again. And spheres of blue radiance. They shot out swiftly from the ships, sped straight toward the *Sunbeam*—and then started circling it. They circled steadily, swiftly, expanding slowly, growing brighter, and staying at a uniform distance from the ship—a distance of about half a mile.

A shell struck one of them, and a shell and blue sphere of radiance vanished together in terrific electric flame. Half a hundred of the strange spheres spun about harmlessly now, and when they came near each other, they shied violently away.

"Wavering planetary paths! That's controlled ball lightning! What I'd give for the secret of that!" gasped Aarn.

"Why isn't it striking us?"

"Circulating in the magnetic field. Say—look!"

The thermometer was rising. It was rising smoothly, and steadily. The room was getting uncomfortably hot, and their own bodies began to get warmer, perspiration stood out on them, and little blue sparks began to jump from bead to bead of that perspiration. Then their keys, their coins, all their metal objects began to have live sparks like a halo about them.

"Damn—ouch—" Aarn reached and held firmly to his controls. "Radio frequency—and plenty. Well—our turn now."

Something hummed vividly in the power room behind. A sudden explosion of air as tremendous power leaped into a transpon beam that smashed its way through the ship's atmosphere.

And a sudden white-hot globule of molten metal where an enemy ship had been.

The hum died, and the air exploded back into the partial vacuum the beam had cut in it.

Again a whine, a clap of thunder, and a blazing white-hot spot of light where a ship had been, exploding light.

"How sweet!" murmured Aarn and swept his deadly probe about through space. He was using no power till the beam met resistance. "It's the transpon beam working in reverse. It's supposed to take the power from a sun for our coils. I'm taking power from the coils, and making miniature suns out of those ships."

Another ship suddenly blazed up and died, and then the remaining ships vanished abruptly as they raced away. The *Sunbeam* had raised its first blisters. Two of the remaining ships began to accelerate gradually, and then moved more rapidly away.

"They aren't all dead yet," said Aarn respectfully. "Those boys make battleships. The darn things are so long, I'd have to melt down two hundred feet of ship before they'd all be gone. And they are supposed to be able to move. You know, I'll bet they haven't got any energy weapon like that transpon beam, and they probably wonder what manner of heat ray I have."

"I thought," said Carlisle, "that you said energy rays—rays that depended on energy for destruction—couldn't be made."

"I did. And I meant it. Figure it out," returned Aarn with a grin.

"I figure," said Spencer, "that the beam is not dangerous—it's what it carries. Does that make any real difference?"

"That's the answer—and it does," replied Aarn. "No sound can be heard three thousand miles away; no sound can cross space; but we can hear sounds which originate on Earth, clear out on Jupiter. How come? The sound doesn't get there—it's carried there by something else. Sound hasn't the penetrative power of radio.

"In this case, a beam can't be handled by a projector if that beam is so destructive to the matter of a ship. But now we have the transpon beam which doesn't destroy—it's quite a harmless little thing, perfectly innocent. Only somebody poured poison in it. It conducts.

"Here's an illustration of the case. Take that piece of wire there—a piece of copper. I can truly and safely say that a wire as thin as the lead of a pencil can't be made the shaft of a machine carrying ten thousand horse power twenty miles. Impossible! But that doesn't mean that ten thousand electric horse power can't be conducted through it. As a driving shaft, as direct mechanical energy in other words, it would be impossible. As a conductor for a second-hand energy, it is possible.

"In general, the only effective rays possible as weapons will be in two classes, the catalyst rays, and the conductor rays.

"By catalyst rays, I mean rays which cause effects at a distance, not by doing work but by giving the signal. A radio beam that releases the explosion of a ton of dynamite might come under that class. A death ray would also come under that class. A ray which set up interference such that the fleet could not communicate, and hence the signals were misunderstood, would also be a catalyst-type beam.

"The conductor beams are, of course, such beams as the transpon.

"The enemy have retired in disgrace. What next? Where do we go from here?"

"Find out where we are first," suggested Spencer.

"The ship's got to be fixed up before we go at all," Carlisle reminded him.

"Oh, I know it! And I know now as much about where we are as I can in less than five years. We are in another space. I know why we are in this particular other space, too. This space is in a sort of strained condition already. Look at the size of the stars we can see. I recognize a number of spectral classes there, and every dog-goned one of them is a supergiant! This is a globular cluster of gigantic stars."

"How can you tell, only glancing at them?" demanded Spencer.

"Experience—I am really guessing, but it is a pretty fair guess. Those spectra look hot. Even allowing for the fact that the light is slightly changed due to different space conditions here."

"And what if they are supergiants, why does that explain anything?"

"We got here by passing through the wall of our space, into a sort of fifth-dimensional interspace. From that interspace we had to enter some other normal four-dimensional space, because we weren't normal to that space at all. Then we took to the one which was easiest of entry—this one, which is strained almost to the breaking point in spots, itself, or at least far nearer that point than any other normal space.

"Those enormous stars simply make great strain spots in the fifth-dimensional interspace side of these spaces. Those strains in the surface attracted any unnatural strain in the interspace. Probably anything that leaks through from any of those other spaces ends up in this space."

"Why near this particular star, then?" asked Spencer. "By the way, I haven't seen it, and I'm going back to look."

"You needn't. It's just a bright spot, and you couldn't tell a thing. I'm going to take some readings presently, and send out a sunbeam and get some results. I've started warming up the tapper tubes. If my suspicions are correct, this is a huge star, far larger than the average, even here. That particular strain spot attracted us."

"Why didn't we land in the star then?"

"What threw us through here? A collision? Do you think we went through just so we could have another and be sent back? Naturally we rolled off the sides of that star's field to some extent before breaking in here."

"Then this is the biggest star in this space of supergiant stars! Wheeee—"

"No; it doesn't have to be at all, Russ," replied Aarn. "It is probably the nearest-biggest star in this space to the side of our own space through which we came. Get it?"

Aarn was working over his instruments now, making adjustments and readings. Gradually a look of puzzled amazement came over his face. More and more carefully he made adjustments. At last he sighed gently and looked up.

"Sweet stellar cycles! It's a Cephid variable or I'm an asteroid. And it's a Cephid of a class you and I never even heard about. Russ, you must be right. That must be the largest star in this whole darned space of supergiants. It is a Cephid with a period that can't be more than a few hours at the outside; it's tremendous. It's gigantic. Maybe it isn't a Cephid, but a different kind of variable that's twice as big.

"I took a radiation measurement on it, and at our present distance it's about as strong as sunlight, but the maximum is in the blue range. Then I took a gravity reading on it and a few other readings—electronic and magnetometric.

"The answer seems to be that that little foot warmer is about one hundred million times as bright and potent as old Sol! We are ten thousand units from that sun's center! About that is to say, ten thousand times one hundred million miles, or about one million million miles. In round figures, at a distance of one trillion miles, this sun is as hot as ours is at a distance of a hundred million. Shall we lay an egg on its surface?"

"Great orbits! How big is the thing?" gasped Spencer.

"It's hard to say." Aarn sighed. "I'd like to know accurately, and will, of course, later, but all I can do is estimate from the known effect of the gravity decline. It seems to be of the order of five hundred million miles in diameter at present and growing larger."

"Larger than Antares—" said Spencer softly.

"But Antares isn't as bad as this, man. Antares is old. Its surface temperature is so low it doesn't compete. It has a temperature of about three thousand. That thing—Heaven alone knows what the temperature is. I can't tell after the light has struggled out against that gravitational field. That field must drag it back through six shades of blue."

"How do we get power? Tap that thing? Say, the Sun is a mild little old dry cell, plugging along peacefully. That's a dynamic, roaring, pulsating furnace."

"We can tap anything," said Aarn firmly. "I've already started the beam."

"How—when do we get power? Next year?"

Aarn sat slowly upright and looked at his friend in horrified surprise. "I didn't stop to think. One trillion miles! Over fifteen hundred hours!" Aarn's face paled slowly. "We're stuck unless—" He fell silent and thoughtful.

"Are there any planets?" Carlisle interrupted him.

"Eh—planets?" Aarn looked up, annoyed. "Dozens. Couldn't separate their effects."

"Dozens?" gasped Spencer. "What kind of a system is this?"

"Those planets," said Aarn, "were probably the throw-offs, the bits of matter swept out by the natural antigravitational fields. On stars that size, there must be billions of tons of stuff thrown off every week. That stuff gets swept up and turns into planets. Probably, though, the process actually is kept going by frequent passages of near-stars. In a globular cluster, where the distances between stars aren't more than a light-year or two, and the darned things have gravitational control extending for nearly that far, the effects would be rather powerful, and more continuous.

"We are probably moving in an orbit such as a meteor might follow, else we'd be bathed in them. I'll bet worlds here have a constant shower that's worse than the Leonids or any other shower back home."

"Nice place for space ships."

"What of it? You can't change things. Look—that star there. I swear I can see a disk, and it's so bright I can scarcely look at it."

"Sunlight from the sun is coming in—we're turning," said Carlisle almost simultaneously.

A stream of almost liquid blue blight cascaded through one of the ports in a thin, thin crescent, and struck the opposite wall. A bright, harsh blue competed with the gas-glow lights.

"If we want to get away from here before those ships go home and tell mamma, we'd better do some work," suggested Aarn. "Canning," he called, "how you making out?"

"This cockeyed, misbegotten inspiration of a half-baked imbecile has more misconceived and willfully aborted circuits than a centipede with locomotor ataxia," Canning roared back. "Come here and see if you can figure it out; I'm about through."

"Spencer, will you take that over? I've got some things I want to do," said Munro. "Want to make some calculations."

"Right enough. But what calc have you in mind?"

"How to go faster than light." Munro grinned and vanished toward the rear.

"All right; don't tell me if you don't want to," snapped Spencer.

----◦----

Munro found Canning engaged in trying to replace the various pieces of apparatus he had been forced to remove to get at the defective circuit. The actual repair had been made, and within twenty minutes he'd have it back together. Then would come the delicate task of tuning the device.

Hour after hour passed as the two engineers struggled over it, and Carlisle and Aarn, both excellent mathematicians, struggled over the math machines.

They had got their first glimpse of the sun when they went back to the calculation room, a bright blue disk, little larger than some of the very near and very large stars.

"There must be two," replied Munro, "two, or more. Those ships were loaded for b'ar, and that means either they were pirates preying on commercial interplanetary shipping, or police, after any strange craft, or more probably, warships.

"Either of the first two presupposes other space craft. There are no space ships if they have no goal. Hence, two worlds. War rockets for planetary war wouldn't be attacking strange ships millions of miles from home. Interplanetary war is indicated.

"Further: They are near-by planets, because of the size of this system. Do you realize that those planets must have orbits with circumferences of the order of three trillion, one hundred and forty-six billion miles?"

"Interplanetary war wouldn't last a year here!" Carlisle laughed.

"Hmmm—maybe it would last that long, if it wasn't too active—if the two forces were too nearly matched. Remember a year, though, would be about eighty thousand of our years."

"But the planets would get so far apart! If they were on opposite sides of their orbits, the contestants would have to quit. Suppose we were fighting Mars, and Mars got on the other side of the Sun. We'd probably declare a temporary peace."

"Yes; true enough. But if Neptune and Pluto were fighting, it would be a thousand years before one would get on the opposite side of the Sun. Here the case is even more extreme, because the difference in their orbits is so small a per cent."

They set to work while the blue disk of the sun crept slowly across their port, and "sank" on the other side. Martin declared a meal, and announced it, while still Spencer and the too-optimistic Canning labored over the job that was to have taken four hours.

After the meal Aarn seemed strangely pleased as he considered the results of the mathematics. Carlisle had performed a number of derivations for him, but had not understood the meaning of the results, as had Munro.

"What is it that's so pleasing?" asked he, at length.

"A chance to go places," replied Munro with a laugh. "I have some apparatus to make. Canning can have that job, while I finish his."

"All right by me, I assure you. My job is distinctly discouraging," snorted Canning.

Aarn grinned, and showed the mechanician-engineer what he wanted made. The man became more and more puzzled as he examined the pattern.

At last he said: "I can make the thing, but darned if I can see why."

"I can," said Munro simply. And that was that.

In half an hour the physicist had done what the engineers had been unable to accomplish, for, when he applied himself, Munro could do delicate work. The circuits were balanced, and he tried them out a bit. The ship moved gently and turned about.

In another hour the simple-complex device Aarn had requested was made. It looked, and was, mechanically simple, but its theoretical implications were enormous.

"Now that you have it, what have you?" asked Spencer.

"Mahomet's decision." Munro grinned.

"Oh, blazes, what is it?" snapped Spencer.

"Mahomet's decision," replied Aarn evenly.

An alarm chose that minute to make its presence known. Aarn jumped. "Great Jupiter—they're back. I'll bet papa and big brother Bill are along to—"

He was out of hearing in the control room. In an instant he was in his seat. A far-flung screen of magnetic force had been disturbed by the approach of a fleet of eight ships. Two were recognizable as the undamaged members of the late adversary. The rest were new.

They were of two new types. The long needle shape was missing in them, and promptly Aarn realized he was seeing now space cruisers and battleships. The two little destroyers led the way, darting rapidly from side to side. Slower, four greater cruisers came up, and behind them two great battleships.

Spencer gasped. "Great planets and little asteroids! It's a battle fleet."

"The destructive beam. They must want the secret of that thing. We're sunk. I'll bet those battleships have noses of ten-foot steel, and the walls for a hundred feet back must be the same," Aarn replied.

A great battleship turned slightly askew, and they got a glimpse of its length. It was a full thousand feet in length, with a series of projecting turrets along her sides and top.

"What a monster—and two of them." Spencer stared aghast.

"The cruiser's not bad," said Munro judiciously.

It wasn't; it was perhaps six hundred feet long, with fewer and smaller turrets, but still a far, far different thing from the destroyer.

As yet the enemy was looking over the *Sunbeam* with caution.

"I wish," said Aarn, "that the aggie coils were full. I'll have to start carving on that battleship, or they won't believe me, and if the thing is all metal, they may be able to get rid of the heat. If it is by any chance silver, we're sunk before we start."

Munro had been busy. With a sudden flick of his finger, a series of relays shot home, and suddenly great beams clapped into action behind him somewhere. And on the bow of the great battleship appeared a spot of flaming, white-hot incandescence. It grew and spread, and the ship jerked wildly.

A great mass of white-hot metal was thrown off by the motion of the ship, and a pit five feet across and two feet deep was left. The beam found lodgment again, and again the metal burned white-hot.

The enemy fleet went into action with their heating rays, their greatest guns, and far greater lightning balls. No results, because of the magnetic atmosphere, from any save the induction ray. The *Sunbeam* became unbearable.

Aarn shifted his attack from the almost-impregnable battleship to the nearest cruiser. A five-foot hole appeared in her side, drove swiftly straight through her interior, and smashed its way to her power compartment inside of fifteen seconds. The control cable had been severed before the ship could be moved, and before a second control could be brought into action, the power storage was reached.

The cruiser disintegrated in the most frightful burst of sheer blue-white incandescence the solarites had ever witnessed. Enormous chunks of flying metal smashed their way through everything within range—save the magnetic atmosphere and the terrific walls of the battleships.

One destroyer was riddled and rolling away, a lifeless hulk. A cruiser was wounded and moved hastily away.

Momentarily, the attack on the *Sunbeam* was stopped. The terrific heat did not abate, but the painful, continuous electric sparks did.

"It's a wonder our circuits don't go dead under that," said Spencer.

"Too much metal—too much grounding—too much shielding of every sort," snapped Aarn.

He spun his controls, lined up his beam, and let go at another cruiser. A white-hot needle smashed its way through the outer wall of two-foot steel, and an inner wall of one-foot steel, and was messing up a kitchen within, when the ship darted away.

"Our coils will be dead in about one and a half minutes." Aarn sighed. "Once I've discharged them—"

He lined up his beam and let it go again. This time the damaged battleship received the dose where it had been hurt before. The metal incandesced and exploded outward in a stream of white-hot sparks. The beam punished its way through an inner one-foot wall and ate a channel straight through the heart of the great ship in a matter of split seconds, for under that terrific drive, a wall of metal only an inch or two thick meant almost nothing at all.

It struck the engine room. To do so, it ate its way through another one-foot wall, but something was the matter, and the great ship was unable to move. The engine room of the battleship was suddenly an inferno of white heat that spread like a widening pool, eating at the heart of the ship. A dozen trapdoors all over the ship opened, and tiny forms shot out into space, making swiftly for other ships.

"I hope they retire," said Aarn wistfully. "We've got about enough power left to cook dinner, and I'd hate to use that up too."

And then—from somewhere behind—something white and gleaming, a long slim body, roared forward. It was twenty-five feet long, and not a foot in diameter, but it had a rocket motor, and it had intentions of damage. It missed the nose of the battleship, which was still in good condition, by about two feet and a skillful maneuver, and struck the injured battleship. A series of explosions that lasted a full thirty seconds followed, and when they were over, the rocket torpedo had eaten a hole through the four-foot armor and was floundering about inside the ship.

A flock of those torpedoes was flying now, and all directed toward the attacking cruisers and battleship. Shells seemed to be invisibly on their way, for huge gouts of white flame sprang up all over the great metal walls, and pits appeared. Occasionally a trapdoor was found, and then a great pit appeared, which was immediately the target for a hundred shells.

The attacking battleship had evidently had more than enough. It retired rapidly, and for the first time the solarites saw their rescuers.

Four great battleships, eight cruisers, and a fleet of destroyers. Every one of those ships was shaped almost exactly like the *Sunbeam* herself, with lines distinctly at variance with those of the other fleet's ships.

"Now what?" asked Spencer in a tired voice. "Do we fight or what?"

"We what," replied Aarn. "They must be friends. They evidently consider any enemy of their enemies a friend. Very useful frame of mind. Probably just as interested in finding out how in the name of blazes we burned holes in that battleship as the enemy were. We've got to signal. How? They don't know what's a beam of destruction and what's a beam of light. And we haven't any more power to argue with, except for what's in the indispensable magnetic atmosphere."

"Can't we signal from—"

"Ah—power!" interrupted Munro, with a smile of pleasure. "That's an easy signal of friendship."

"What is it? That we've got power?"

"No; that we haven't. The man you do a favor for," said Aarn, working rapidly, "is twice your friend."

<hr />

The lights aboard the *Sunbeam* began to fade slowly, growing dimmer and dimmer. A searchlight reached out suddenly from the solarian ship and died slowly in redness as the lights faded rapidly to darkness. The strangers watching from outside saw a number of small bobbing lights move about inside the ship. Presently a doorway opened, and a light, a dim, dim light shot out in a curve, something trailing along behind it like a tail.

A destroyer maneuvered cautiously over to it and picked up the dim light and the trailing thing. It was an incandescent bulb. The trailing thing was a piece of twisted pair wire, the wires connected to the bulb. It was a very dim bulb. It told a long, and complete story to the highly intelligent men of the Magyan ships.

It said in brief: This ship uses electric power. It has used all its power in fighting, so thoroughly that even the lights have failed. This wire has been tossed over to us that we may supply power. It gives us a means of measuring the voltage of their power system, determining whether they want a.c. or d.c., and many other things are suggested, such as the fact that the stranger ship is indeed in trouble and lost.

The Magyan destroyer captain consulted his superiors, while his engineers made tests on the wire. The voltage they determined. It was about a hundred and eighty-six, on our scale. They then connected the light bulb to a source of potential, and ran it up till the bulb was glowing at the greatest safe temperature. The voltage they used in this was two hundred and thirty. Therefore they pumped over current at two hundred and thirty volts.

Immediately the lights on board the *Sunbeam* flashed up once more, and three solarites gave a cheer of joy.

"Step number one!" called Carlisle.

"We've got to talk to them. Let's hope their language isn't too hard," mourned Spencer. "I never was good at languages."

"I think I'd better stay here," said Aarn, "and finish fixing this boat. You'll have to go over there— Whoa, someone is coming. Spence, take the control room. I'm working in the air lock, and I intend to pass that bird right into the lounge. Meet him there."

For the first time the solarians got a view of a Magyan. Anto Rayl was to be a friend to them. He was six feet tall, and absolutely human in every character.

His eyes were gray, with speckles of golden color floating in them, his face was tanned deeply, a lean, strong face with wide, high cheek bones, a straight, thin nose with delicate nostrils, his chin firm and short in front, with a straight bang across the back of his neck.

His uniform was some woven-elastic fiber that evidently was capable of stretching in all directions. It fitted him closely, revealing a body that was muscular and well-proportioned. His chest was deep and wide, and his bones strong.

He looked at the Terrestians interestedly and with some peculiar anxiety and surprise. His eyes darted swiftly around the power room, and a slight look of disappointment came into them, for absolutely nothing was readable to him now, since all the mechanisms were covered, as understandable as an automobile with the hood down.

Then suddenly he noticed the form of the Jovian, half hidden where he had been opening the lock door.

The Magyan slowly pulled a tiny metal tab, and the absolutely transparent envelope that had protected him in his short trip across space fell away. He was still looking at the Jovian, and at last turned away, a distinct look of displeasure on his face. Aarn was himself annoyed by this—then suddenly grinned widely. He laughed softly, and the Magyan turned toward him.

Aarn stepped forward with a friendly smile and stretched out a hand. With a slight smile, Aarn shook hands, keeping his fingers flaccid. The Magyan would learn the Jovian's strength later.

"Greetings, friend, and you sure fill the definition of a good one!"

"*Ahtop ah-menahep—etran matral hepanet.*"

"Hmm—we won't get anywhere that way. Look," said Aarn distinctly. "I'm—Aarn."

"Aarn?"

"Yes—Aarn. He—Russ. He—Car."

"Ahm—Ahm—Aarn—Russ—Cah."

"That's it. Who are you?"

"Anto Rayl," replied the Magyan.

"Anto Rayl. Good! Now to learn a language. It had better be theirs if we possibly can. Let's see. How can I ask?"

Spencer smiled. "Easy!" He picked up a chair that was near by, held it before him, and pointed with his other hand. "Chair," he said distinctly. "What?" he inquired.

For a moment Anto Rayl was puzzled; then he grasped the idea. In a moment he had pulled a small instrument from his pocket and was talking rapidly. Aarn looked at the thing closely and reached forward and pushed it away from him. He shook his head, and then put a hand to the instrument. His hand undulating, he moved it across the room till it struck the metal wall, then he simply smashed his hand flat against the metal.

"No. Won't go."

It wasn't the metal. It was the magnetic atmosphere, but there was a wall which radio wouldn't penetrate easily.

In an hour, a teacher had come from one of the other ships, a skillful artist. He, with Anto Rayl, started teaching them, and evidently Anto Rayl's people didn't know the meaning of fatigue, for they kept at it for ten hours straight. And it was a pure, intensive course. So intensive, and so purely lingual, that absolutely no information passed.

In the meantime a heavier cable had been run in from one of the battleships, and the great aggie coils of the *Sunbeam* were slowly being charged. However, Anto Rayl did stop once to inquire where in the name of something or other all the power was going to. It seemed that about one quarter of the battleship's power had been sent over, and that was all they could spare.

Aarn grinned and took Anto Rayl to one of the doors in the wall of the *Sunbeam*. Behind was one single group of coils. Aarn pointed to them, and indicated they were about one tenth full. Then he pointed to another group barely visible, and indicated they had no charge at all. Anto looked incredulous.

The labor of learning a language, even passably, is terrific. It is so great that the author of fiction invariably is tempted to resort to telepathy as a short cut. Aarn and his friends retired with the firm conviction that some such thing was badly needed. All they seemed to have learned was an incredible number of words, such simple words as "go" and "away" and "be" and such, and they realized that they could not so much as give a sensible sentence. "The chair is up there," was about their limit.

"At any rate," said Spencer with a groan, his head between his hands, "they don't go in for declensions, conjugations, and dual, plural, and singular voices, and there seems to be some rhyme and reason in some of it, anyway."

"Maybe," said Carlisle disgustedly. "Also a headache."

Martin had breakfast ready when they awoke in the morning, and Canning announced that he had finished the connections Aarn had prescribed for the new apparatus.

Anto Rayl was not back yet and did not show up when their activity began. Aarn went over Canning's connections and tested them carefully. Next he took some power readings and determined that he had enough power for what he wanted to accomplish.

"This," he said with a smile, "will surprise our friends immensely. It will also surprise you."

"It will," agreed Spencer. "You haven't yet told your employer what you have been doing."

"My employer has become merely a supernumerary here." Aarn smiled. "We are about to go to the mountain, if you must know."

"You mentioned that," replied Spencer. "I took it to mean that since Anrel—as Anto Rayl called the sun here—won't come out along your beam in anything less than half a year or so, you plan going there. Fine! Just tell me, though, how, in the sacred name of the nine known planets, you expect to accomplish that which every physicist since Einstein has said was impossible."

"None of them said it. We've already done it."

Spencer looked at him silently for a moment. "All right, I am a liar. Now prove it."

"How far is it back to Earth?"

"Uhhh—that's not a distance."

"All right, then. We aren't going a distance. Only we're going to wind up somewhere near that sun," said Aarn, and started putting up the remaining shutters.

All but the ones in the pilot room were up. In a moment only the television served to show them the Magyan patrol about them.

"Well, good-bye," said Aarn.

He depressed a control. Instantly the Magyan patrol became a two-dimensional picture of a Magyan patrol. The battleships were silhouettes, and the whole thing vanished in a puff. The sun, Anrel, alone remained unchanged as minute after minute sped by. Then, at last, even it began to show signs of growth. But something else was growing off to one side—a world that flashed larger and larger, that twisted and turned as their ship fled past it at a velocity that was preposterous, impossible.

"We aren't," explained Aarn, "really going through space. We're going round it and keeping contact rather slightly. We're half out of space. We had just enough power to build up that condition, thanks to the Magyan battleship."

"How fast are we going?" demanded Spencer.

"We aren't," said Munro blankly.

"Grrr—how fast would we be going if we were?"

"About twenty-five hundred times as fast as light. That means that where light would take about fourteen hundred hours, it will take us a bit more than half an hour. We won't go all the way, though. I'm stopping several million miles short. And making another slight modification in space as soon as I get the power."

The system was simple enough, when understood. The ship, in crossing from one normal space to the other, was in an interspace where it did not belong, and was instantly shoved to a place it could exist. In being pushed through that strange interspace, the meaning of distance was forgotten. It could have alighted anywhere in the other space. Aarn was intentionally shoving himself halfway out of the normal space into that interspace, and then coming back where he wished.

Anrel grew larger. The great blue-fire disk grew with astonishing slowness, for they were covering billions and hundreds of billions of miles with every second. But the titanic sun was so distant, that, even so, change was slow.

"That's about enough," Munro said at last, when Anrel was a disk of blue fire that spread over half the firmament, blotting everything else from sight.

The television eye was cut down to a minimum, and a diversion-shunt circuit called into play to handle the enormous influx of energy. The temperature of the ship was rising rapidly even here in the interspace condition.

"Look out!" warned Aarn.

He cut a switch. Instantly he threw a second. In that momentary lapse of time, the shutter before their eyes had grown red-hot, and the television screen was blank.

"Radiation!" Spencer exclaimed and fell silent.

God's mighty experimental laboratories, the suns of space, made the weapons of humankind seem futile. The mere exhaust energy of this star had nearly fused that heavy metal shutter in a fraction of a second.

"What's cooling us?" Spencer asked at length.

Aarn was silent—and busy. "I'd like to know this sun's frequencies better—"

"What's this mean?" asked Carlisle.

"It means I may hook onto about a million times as much energy as I want," replied Munro. "And we aren't being cooled. I worked this out from the same interspace idea. That interspace experience was a great thing for me." He grinned. "I've made the ship invisible."

"Invisible?" gasped Carlisle. "I can see it—"

"Certainly, defect. But it's invisible from outside. I've shunted the incident electromagnetic energy through ninety degrees into gravitomagnetic energy, and back again on the other side. We aren't absorbent to gravitomagnetic radiation, and it passes right through."

"Gravitomagnetic—what's that?"

"Electromagnetic energy is energy which is cyclicly transformed from an electric field to a magnetic field and back again, and possesses the property of traveling as radiation through space at a speed of a hundred and eighty-six thousand miles per second. Gravitomagnetic energy is the same, except that the change is between gravitational and magnetic fields."

"Does it occur in nature?"

"Naturally."

"Why hasn't it been detected and used before this?" asked Spencer.

"I just gave the reason. It passes through any physical body unhindered. Only certain force fields can detect and handle it. I detected it against my gravitational fields, naturally. It won't go very far, anyway, before it gets broken up into a different form of energy. I think it's the source of cosmic rays. Gravitational fields tend to combine, and unlike electromagnetic radiation which always goes down the scale, gravitomagnetic radiation is willing to go up the scale.

"That beam ought to be getting near the surface layer now. I've got it cut down to nothing. I hope it leaves me something either of the power or the ship." Aarn read his instruments carefully.

"Anyway, here is the result. I can get near this sun, by-pass the radiation, and live to tell about being here."

"Is the television burned out?" asked Carlisle. "I'd like to watch that star."

"I just got through saying that the light and heat were by-passed," said Aarn patiently. "We can't see out. I can make a small hole in the screen if I want to, and I'd not live long enough to close it."

"Will this invisibility be useful in fighting! Oh, oh! We'll have some fun with the—Tefflans, Anto Rayl called them."

"Wrong," replied Aarn, his eyes on the instruments. "They'd spot this field a billion miles away, when they couldn't see us at all if we were in normal space. That beam is just—about—here."

He waited expectantly, the whole ship quiet in suspense. Still minutes passed.

"It didn't get anywhere at the outer layer," said Aarn softly. "It's going deeper."

———❦———

A deafening explosion echoed through the ship, a tremendous glare of blue light that burned through it, a deep-throated hum of rushing power that made the entire ship vibrate with its beat. Rapidly Aarn was cutting down the power.

"Everything's—full—nearly."

The power died, the blue glare faded gradually, and finally was gone.

"Done!" Aarn sighed as he cut his beam. "Got a stock of power now that counts, and I'm going to have more shortly. If we want to get back, Russ, we'll have to rip out some of those nice extra bedrooms and the lounge, and the lab will have to be filled with coils. That lab can be set up on Magya, and we can work from there as a base. It may be years before we get back, for we've got a thousand observations to make. We've got to find our own particular space to get back to. It has no extra-great tension so that we can find it easily."

The ship seemed to reel, then suddenly the television was working again; it showed the star spinning across the screen, then rapidly retreating as they headed back to the Magyan patrol.

"How will you find our space?" asked Spencer after a moment of horrified thought. He'd not thought of that angle.

"Take a chance, largely, if necessary. The quickest way home, if it will work, is to go after the space fields of antigravitor apparatus. We know they have that on Earth, and it isn't like a natural field, so we know intelligent beings live there.

"But they may not be our intelligent beings, and we may simply land in third space. There may be a way to localize the thing, though.

"But first—I'm interested in the Magyans. I noticed something you may not have done. What's their word for mother?"

"Matra," replied the puzzled engineer.

"Father?"

"Paldri."

"That's the thing I noticed. Just think. See if it isn't a series. Padre-pater-paternal-Vater-father-pere-paldri. And madre-mater-mutter-mere-mother matra. I swear those similarities are not chance. There were others I noticed. That is an Earth-human race. They were perfectly, absolutely human. You saw that.

"We're getting back to that squad now, and I'm going to learn their story. They're too human to be anything else. And this is the place where anything cast adrift from the planet would inevitably land. I want to hear that story—and about those Tefflans. I saw—one of them. Did you?"

"Saw one? When?"

"In the battle. It was red. And—it wasn't human. I hated it at sight. It was—a devil! Tail—horns—"

CHAPTER VII

ANTO RAYL, EYED THEM uncertainly as he entered with the artist-teacher. "Where did you go?" he asked.

"To the sun," replied Aarn, almost as surprised to find he could answer as to the fact that Anto had asked an intelligible intelligent question in the new language.

"You went red, then went black, then went out of seeing," said Anto Rayl.

"You can make sense with those fool words we learned yesterday," said Carlisle.

"We went to the sun. The sun is far. We went fast. We went more fast than light, so we went out of seeing," Aarn answered Anto.

Anto looked puzzled. His question was quite evident to the Jovian. He was puzzled, because he knew that nothing could go faster than light, and because these men were learning the language. Now the strangers might be able to do the impossible; on the other hand they certainly could get mixed up in their language.

Aarn spoke again; "We went fast—very very, very more fast. So fast that light was slow. It went red, then more fast, and it went black, so we went out of seeing."

Anto smiled his understanding. "Why?"

Aarn explained briefly, and with every word and phrase his surprise and shock grew. He found himself talking a sort of pidgin language that consisted principally of basic, simple ideas such as go, be, live, die, power, fast, slow, heat, cold, air, and such, and a number of modifiers. The result was a language which lacked all signs of beauty or nobility, but had every possible desirability as a quickly, easily learned language. One did an enormous amount of "going" and "being" but the result was intelligible.

To attempt to maintain the peculiar jerky style of that simple but ungraceful language is useless. In giving Anto Rayl's story I abandon it completely for the English translation which gives the thought, not the words.

Anto Rayl listened with astonishment to Munro's description of the source of the *Sunbeam's* power. He gaped in amazement, and stared with a new respect at the hulking form of the antigravity field. No ship of theirs had ever attempted to approach the sun, not only because of the terrific distance—so great that it would have taken a lifetime almost for a space ship going at any safe speed—but because of the terrific gravitational field.

"Doesn't that enormous energy burn out that coil? If it contains energy sufficient to lift this ship those trillions of miles against the terrible gravity of Anrel, I should expect it to be consumed," he said wonderingly.

"It doesn't contain the power. That's the point. Quite the opposite. It keeps the space around it from containing that energy. It prevents the energy's existence. Therefore it contains none and is under no strain."

"But the power coils?"

"An altogether different thing. They build up a field instead of tearing one down."

"But tell us your story. We feel sure that your race and ours are blood kin. How can this be? We came through the wall that leads from space to space."

"Many, many, millias—periods of a thousand-thirty-hour-days—ago, in a world on the other side of the Wall of Naught, our forefathers lived," said Anto Rayl. "It was a green world about the size of Magya, but slightly smaller, and made up of fair lands and broad seas. And in the middle of the greatest sea of all, lived the Ma-jhay-anhu, the mother race.

"They built great cities, carved great monuments on their broad, flat continent, and developed a great civilization. They were a people who roamed little, who multiplied slowly, and they did not search the world and colonize it widely. As their ships grew greater, and their air flying machines came, they visited all the continents. In some they found wild savages, hairy and bestial. A different race altogether. They were almost apes. Colonies were not needed, none established.

"Then—the year of the calamity. There was a shaking of the ground, a great cleft appeared in the side of the sacred mount, where lived the rulers of the Ma-jhay-anhu. And from it came the Teff-Hellani. They were—something else, a misbreed; something the processes of life should not have produced. They were, we believed, the result of the evolution of a strange crossing of utterly different races, the primates of the goats. A million years ago, perhaps, these things had been locked under the Earth in a vast system of caverns beneath the continent of Mahu, and in the strange lights of strange elements they developed.

"Their faces were long and narrow, and they had horns, but their eyes and their noses and their mouths were something like those of humans. They had a torso and a pair of true hands, but their feet were the feet of goats and their bodies were hairy. And the strange light had bred something into them that made them red, for the light was greenish in hue. They were hideous. It was hot in those depths, and they loved heat. Only in summer could they endure the outside air. Then they were always hugging great fires.

"But they were intelligent, and their vitality was terrible. They were carnivorous. They captured our people and carried them off, women and children—for meat supplies. They had never had any before. They bred them down there in their foul caverns, and some few escaped to tell of the horrors.

"And the Ma-jhay-anhu fought with more and newer weapons. Those two races hated each other instinctively. They always have. They always will, for that matter.

"The warfare lasted longer than we know, save that it began with arrows and with swords, and ended finally with space ships and deadly rays.

"Tsoo-Ahs was the last great ruler of Ma-jhay-anhu. He saw that never could hope of the end come till the last member of one race or the other was wiped out. Both had airships now, so no colonies had been established, neither the Teff-Hellani nor the Ma-jhay-anhu had dared a small colony. But now Tsoo-Ahs sent thousands of young men and young women into all the corners of the world, hastily, for a plan had been made, and it must be executed before the Teff-Hellani learned of it.

"The expeditions set out—half equipped, uninstructed, without plan. And Tsoo-Ahs, who had invented two great things that were to make this thing possible, set to work. He had learned to extract the secret energy store of the indivisible particle. And he had learned to hurl the deadly ball of electric energy."

"Great glory! Tsoo-Ahs. Zeus!" exclaimed Spencer.

"Naturally. Sit down and shut up. Ever hear of Mu? That's what's left of Mahu. Ever hear of Easter Island and the remains of the great city out in the middle of the Pacific? That's more of Mu—or Mahu. Now shut up and hear how come. Also hear how come Mayans built pyramids and the Egyptians built pyramids and the Babylonians or some race around there built a tower. And why the Greeks and other races kept showing and talking about human heads on inhuman bodies," said Aarn.

"Tsoo-Ahs sent messengers to all his kingdom to hold a great feast," Anto Rayl went on. "And while the feast was in progress, and there was great merry-making, and all laws and restrictions were relaxed, for he knew that all must die, Tsoo-Ahs began his work. He had made five great ships of a wonderful new kind which need no wings and could go far beyond the air. And he sent them up over the great crevice that was the entrance to the kingdom of the Teff-Hallani.

"The ships began a bombardment which fused the rock and split it open. The great crevice spread more and more and presently an army of the Teff-Hellani swarmed up, and an air fleet, but the army was annihilated and the air fleet blown out of the air, and the great crevice widened, and stretched half a mile nearer to the blue-deep waters of the great sea.

"And just as the waters of the sea roared suddenly downward into the mouth of the great caverns, a ship shot out, a ship not unlike our own, and it spit forth a series of great torpedoes that shot forward and buried themselves in the sides of four of the ships of the Ma-jhay-anhu, and the four ships were destroyed.

"A fifth torpedo was fired, but the skillful ones aboard the remaining ship dodged it, and sent a lightning bolt toward the Teff-Hellani ship. The Teff-Hellani was forced to flee. His guns made no impression, and the light-ning balls pursued him. His torpedoes were exhausted, and now, so great a volume of water flowed down the mighty mouth of the sunken caverns, the ship could not re-enter, but could only watch and attempt to stop the flow. It was hopeless.

"In an hour the world shook, and the vast continent of Mahu settled some-what. Tsoo-Ahs had expected that, for he knew. Worlds are made of blocks, like many huge boats floating close together in water. When one block gets too heavy, it will sink. Mahu had been balanced. She was full of great caverns, but her rocks were very heavy. Then the caverns were filled with quintillions of tons of water, and Mahu grew heavy, and the great continent sank.

"She sank and sank, till only the tops of a few volcanoes protruded, and then the violent action that shook the whole world took place.

"And now, remember, there remained two ships capable of fighting in the emptiness beyond worlds, the ship of the Teff-Hellani, and the remaining ship of the Ma-jhay-anhu. Now the five ships of the Ma-jhay-anhu were intended to have carried the last load of colonists to the five great colonies, and they were to have been the means of communication, and they carried tools and supplies and seeds.

"But four were destroyed, and the fifth was busy—busy seeking that last ship of the Teff-Hellani.

"They got on the trail of that ship, at last, by means of an instrument whose nature we cannot understand, and they followed it, faster and faster—faster—and each was protected by a powerful force that hurled meteors from its path, a reversing of the effect of gravity.

"They engaged in battle, and the Teff-Hellani had the advantage because their shells would pierce the protective meteor shield and were attracted to their victim by some means, while the ball-lightning was not attracted but tended to follow only a straight line, while the Teff-Hellani dodged about.

"Both were too busily engaged. Across the small expanse on that little planetary system they had chased and fought, and now an incredibly rugged and dark mass of matter—a broken fragment of a world—loomed before them. Both struck it.

"They were separated when they discovered themselves in this strange space. They each hoped the other was dead—destroyed. The space was too great. They could not locate themselves. Their ships were damaged, and each sought a planet.

"We know of eighty-seven planets which revolve around this sun. There are more. And each of those two ships landed on a different planet. The Teff-Hellani picked one nearer the sun—warmer. But they could not get the warmth they wanted before their ship would give out, for this system is too vast. So they chose the planet we know as Teff-el. Our forefathers chose the planet we know as Magya.

"The people were in a peculiar situation. They had started out to colonize, but not in such a place. They had expected many other people to aid them. Fortunately there were both males and females in the ship, so that life should not die, but there were no teachers, no thinkers, and no mechanicians. They were able to make, when they had tools and power to work with, and supplies of metal and chemicals. But they did not know how to find those supplies. They never had to.

"In a generation the ship was a temple where the children worshipped the knowledge of the forefathers of the old world, blindly. Then, as generations passed, a stone temple was built about the now-ruined ship. Finally the stone temple crumbled from neglect, and the Magyans spread over their planet as savages, but never totally lost to knowledge, for the legends persisted. And gradually civilization roused itself once more and grew, and the legends were thought of only as foolish sayings, tales for children, and disregarded, the ancient ideas of gods and goddesses—superstition.

"Ten hundred millia ago a man crossed space. He went to the nearest of our four moons. Then he went to the outermost. A crude rocket device. Again the thing was done. Then a ship finally took off from the fourth moon and went to the nearest planet. It was to have taken a millia. The ship never returned, but another went. It did not return. The third did not. The fourth came back, its rockets exhausted, and three greater rockets closed on its heels. It was a greatly improved model, or it would never had escaped as it did, nor lasted so long in the chase. Signals had preceded it, so there were half a dozen other rockets out to meet it, and the convoy drove off the rockets which had pursued across five hundred million miles of space.

"Fortunately, the rockets which went out to rescue the hard-pressed inter-planetary rocket were a new experimental type. They were very swift and very agile. The Tefflan rockets were equipped with guns. Our rockets had none, but one clever rocket-pilot had a man stand in the air lock with a space suit on, and throw heavy crates and castings about."

"The pilot headed his rocket straight for the enemy, then just short of a crash he changed his course abruptly, the heavy castings smashed their way straight on and ruined the ship. The others tried the same thing. One ship was punctured and died. The others retired hastily.

"The returned rocket explorer, Harn Malto, told what had happened. The others had landed on Teff-el and been killed instantly. For the Tefflans had their ancient legends as we had ours, and they, too, had seen in the humans the hated enemy. Harn Malto saw in the Tefflans the hated enemy of legend.

"The legends revived. And war rockets were made instantly. Some wild terrorist shouted that the cities would be destroyed and only underground was it safe. A man by the name of Hero Shal arose. He made a device which would crumble rock—a peculiar slow-explosion torpedo. He could dig his way into the hardest rock with amazing speed. The thing exploded grain by grain, only one grain at a time, but all in less than a second. It shattered rock, and the stuff came out dust. He was of course accused of attempting to advertise his product.

"Six tiny Tefflan scout rockets dropped noiseless and lightless from the sky, and wiped out Mag-harun, our largest city, in thirty-five seconds. The scout ships were piloted by Tefflans who went uncomplaining to suicide. Each was a five-ton missile of metallic sodium, which exploded and cast the flaming, liquid metal all over the city. The entire city was a single sheet of flame in seconds. Thousands and tens of thousands died through fire; as many more were killed by the poisonous, consuming dust that rose from the burning sodium.

"It happened that Hero Shal had lived and built his underground home there. He was unharmed, and, when the blazing ruins cooled, walked out.

"In a month cities were drilling their way underground; war rockets were being equipped with the deadly Shal torpedoes. Nothing could stop them. Even today the mightiest battleship armor frequently falls before them if they are not torn loose in time."

"Was that what we saw used?" interrupted Aarn.

"Yes. Those first rockets carried small ones, propelled by compressed springs. When the Tefflans came again, they destroyed another city, but there were few people in it, for, thanks to the wonderful Shal-crumbling bombs, great underground cities had been dug. They were half a mile below the surface. We had descended even as the original Tefflan race.

"And our archaeologists were seeking that ancient temple. Millias passed in unavailing search, while the rockets grew more and more deadly. Bases were established on the outer moons, and fortified. They were our centers of defense. And at last a fleet of ten rockets set out for Teff-El. Each rocket carried a tiny scout rocket which was to do most of the fighting.

"That was the expedition of Tarnel Car. There followed expedition after expedition, and gradually the rockets improved.

"Then, only about one hundred years ago, the Tefflans found the remnants of their ancient flyer. They found also the remnants of its engine. The engine had been protected by the very nature of it, and still existed intact. The driving apparatus, the disks, existed also intact, and that was enough. They made one of the new ships. They attacked us when they had three completed, and they destroyed utterly the bases on our moons, they destroyed our fleet, and they tried to destroy our cities.

"But we made little scout cruisers that shot out of hidden holes in the ground at night, careened suddenly toward their huge armored battleships, and loosed a Shal torpedo. They had never learned the secret of the Shal torpedoes, have not yet. They destroy themselves, and are always destroyed in a damaged ship before it is abandoned.

"The Shal torpedoes at last were made large enough so they ate holes in the giant battleships. Then rocket drives were added to the torpedoes so they destroyed the armor and went on drilling through to the inside.

"Shal torpedoes loaded with poisons finally forced the Tefflans off the planet. They set up bases on our moons and began bombarding our cities. They were slowly eating their way inward when a Magyan discovered the secret of atomic energy independently. He was disappointed; it was not what he had hoped for. It has always annoyed us. We require, still, great amounts of fuel, though theory shows that an engine could be made which would require so little a single man could carry it."

"How do you do it?" interrupted Aarn once more.

"The atoms of two metals are mutually destructive in certain conditions. I cannot show you now. It would take too long. The destroyed atoms fly about at tremendous speeds in all directions, the various electrical charges blending in a sort of continuous flame.

"This process is carried on in the center of a great boiler filled with a liquid metal. The flying atom-parts are captured in the metal, stopped, and become only heat and gas. The heat boils the metal and runs turbines; the gas is exhausted into space. But we are still limited, because, while there is a great deal of energy in the fuel, and it comes off as rapidly as we wish, the electric generators are not capable of handling more than a certain load, and are heavy."

"Wouldn't water be better in your boilers than mercury? It isn't so terribly dense," suggested Spencer.

"No; it isn't dense and won't stop the flying ions," Aarn reminded him. "Besides it would be smashed to atoms, literally, and give you something besides steam. Mercury is already smashed to atoms. But continue your story."

"It is short, now," Anto Rayl said. "With atomic power we succeeded in repulsing the Tefflans. We discovered our own ship soon—the ancient one, and the ball-lightning device. Sadly, the Tefflans have learned that secret now. It will be so much longer before the last Tefflan is killed. If only the worlds were nearer that we might fight better and finish this!"

CHAPTER VIII

"I THINK," SAID SPENCER, "that we can tell you what became of the other part of your race—the part that remained behind. The colonists were in terrible condition, because now they had no means of acquiring tools, they had no supplies, they could not communicate, for their planes, I suppose, ran out of fuel quickly, and they had not carried sufficient apparatus to make more.

"They, too, lost their civilization. Now some of those colonists had settled in Europe, as we call it today. They met there a race of terrible savages, short, squat men, incredibly ugly, cannibalistic. They called them 'ogres,' and the myths of that savage race exist still. We know them scientifically as Neanderthals. These ogres were afraid to attack grown men, but they stole children, and some women, but eventually through ages of fighting were wiped out, and civilization grew again.

"And a portion landed in Africa and started a colony in Egypt. There were natives already there, and the natives were not intelligent, so the colonists learned the language of the natives, since the natives were too stupid to learn their language. And the colonists declined through several generations, while dragging the natives out of the utter abyss of ignorance, and then all advanced slowly to a high civilization, till at length the blood of the colonists was overcome by the poorer blood of the many native strains, and the civilization vanished.

"And another group landed in America, and they found natives, as had those who landed in Egypt, and they followed a very similar process, and again the civilization died. In each case, when the blood of the old Ma-jhay-anhu was diluted, it won for a time, then died.

"What happened to the others, I cannot guess. Maybe they landed in India.

"But only the undiluted Ma-jhay-anhu blood lived to reach a civilization once more that endured fairly well.

"And now, Anto Rayl, we have come through the Wall of Naught to join you. We shall go back, but this now is your life, your space, and your world. We shall open up paths of commerce between the worlds, perhaps?" Spencer turned to Munro questioningly.

"Not till we learn how to find our own space," he answered. "That may require years of observation and calculation."

Anto Rayl looked at Munro with interest. "What you need exists, I believe," he said at length. "An old legend: the captain of that ancient Ma-jhay-anhu ship wanted to go back through, and he was a scientist, and he spent many years observing and calculating, and in the end learned what he needed to know. But he found that the ship was no longer capable of making the trip, for parts had decayed in the more than thirty millia that had passed.

"And the Teff-Hellani were exploring and found our world, attacked suddenly, and wiped out half the colony, one of the two cities. And they landed and looted the city, and among the loot was the book of data, inscribed on plates of an alloy of three noble metals which would not rust or decay, nor would change with time, according to the legend. For the old captain was not dead. But he said that the Teff-Hellani scientists would not be able to go through any more than he, but that one day the plates would be recovered from the Teff-Hellani. 'The Plates of the Secret will be recovered, and the last of the Teff-Hellani will be destroyed by a great world.' Those are the words of his prophecy. I do not understand the meaning of the last. But if you need data, I am sure those stolen plates, which we have never troubled to recover, will contain it."

"We've got to get them," snapped Aarn. "It took that old captain nearly a lifetime, and we don't want to wait as long as that!"

"We're with you, Anto Rayl. Those Teff-Hellani might decide to try going back themselves, since we came through," said Spencer grimly.

———◇———

There was a restlessness among the ships of the Magyan squadron, and the great battleships swung slowly around and headed off to one side, towing behind them the massive wreck of the Tefflan battleship. The cruisers swung into position around the monster ships, and the destroyers and smaller craft followed. Only Anto Rayl's ship remained in attendance. A cylinder electromagnet suddenly shot out from it, and fixed itself in the magnetic pole of the *Sunbeam*. Immediately a slight jerk, and the destroyer started off towing the *Sunbeam*.

Aarn grinned as he saw it. "Where's your planet, Anto Rayl?"

Anto Rayl pointed it out, and Aarn made some adjustments. Suddenly the electromagnet shied away, a half dozen instruments on the control panel changed abruptly, the destroyer slipped rapidly to one side, then behind—and held steady. But the spot of light that was Magya was suddenly shifting slowly and steadily.

A flash of light past the windows indicated the battle fleet as the *Sunbeam*, with the destroyer now in tow, swept past.

"By the Lords of Space! How fast are we going? Why was there no acceleration?" exclaimed Anto Rayl.

"I can't explain offhand, Anto Rayl. It depends on a question of the structure of space. We are going rapidly, and every atom of us was accelerated uniformly. This drive is not suitable to your great battleships—that is, we can't install it in those already made, but we can install acceleration neutralizers, and if that space disk you talked about is what I think it is, we can get real speed out of those big fellows. Your people will have to make a lot of things for me," Aarn went on.

Ahead the planet Magya was looming larger, rapidly. And off to one side three moons showed. A dozen huge ships were swinging swiftly around the world to intercept them, and Aarn slowed. A light broke out on the destroyer, a bluish light that winked and trembled rapidly, then died into blackness. Instantly an answering light broke out on one ship below, and the squadron of the home guard swung into a ring formation, and picked up speed as the *Sunbeam* and its escort dropped slowly toward the planet.

The ships were four huge battleships, like those that had come to their rescue out in space, but surrounded by a perfect cloud of small ships, some little larger than torpedoes.

"What different ships does your navy consist of?" Aarn asked Anto Rayl.

"There are six main classes of fighting machines. The great battleships are first, weighing in the neighborhood of one million five hundred thousand tons.

"A battleship is almost indestructible. Even when blown completely in two, it is exceedingly dangerous, as it maintains maneuverability and fighting power. They are armed with the lightning apparatus, one set for each engine. Great guns, with armor-piercing Shal shells; Shal torpedo tubes, gas guns, and induction beams, and every known weapon, in the greatest possible size.

"The heavy battle cruisers come next. Did I say that at present we have a total of fifty-six serviceable battleships? Two are in the Ma-kanee base. That is on our fourth moon. They are being repaired after a battle with the Tefflani. Three more are under construction. We are soon going to start manufacturing four, for a new steel process has made this increase possible. Also, we are now recovering all broken derelicts of space for their metal.

"Of the heavy battle cruisers we have a total of a hundred and five in condition. Twenty-three are in repair docks on Manayo, the third moon. There was a heavy engagement recently that sent them there. The heavy cruisers weigh about five hundred thousand tons, and are equipped with two sets of engines, smaller lightning apparatus, heavy accumulator banks, lighter guns, but numerous torpedo tubes. Their armor is two and a half feet thick, enough to stop heavy shells, but not capable of stopping torpedoes.

"They are half as powerful and a third as heavy as a battleship, so their movements are somewhat more rapid. They are very dangerous craft.

"The next are the light cruisers. We have a hundred and eight of them now in commission. They are much the same as the heavy cruisers, with lighter engines, lighter accumulators, and much lighter armor. Their task is to punish the destroyers.

"We have over five hundred and eighty destroyers, about five thousand scout ships, and about ten thousand spy ships. The destroyers carry a light ball-lightning apparatus."

"I've always read," said Carlisle, "of space fleets meeting with seven thousand battleships from here, and twenty thousand from there, and so on."

"Neglecting," said Spencer, "the fact that a battleship represents something like a hundred million credits of hard cash. It represents a year or more of hard work, over a million tons of steel and a lot of complex apparatus, plus a population running into the thousands.

"How was it, Anto Rayl, that we were able to destroy that Tefflan battleship?"

Anto Rayl smiled, and Aarn was smiling, too.

"The answer is," said the latter, "that we didn't, I suspect."

Anto Rayl nodded. "You didn't. But you hopelessly crippled it. They had already noticed our approach, and being so badly crippled, and expecting a further dose any minute, they left in haste. They didn't know your power was gone."

"It was," said Munro grimly. "It isn't now. I see we seem to have arrived."

They had been shooting over mountains and lakes, over a green world of plains and hills and great blackened, torn bare spots.

"Bombs," Anto Rayl explained. "Radio-active. It will be dead for a century."

Now they had reached the border of a great sea, where a huge mountain range seemed to run off into the water in a series of islands. Their escort had taken the lead, and was hovering over one of the islands now.

Suddenly Aarn gasped, for the tiny blazing sun and the deep violet sky was obscured by a mist that grew more and more dense, a rapidly rising, vapory cloud that swept up from the sea. In a minute the entire district was veiled in an impenetrable fog. Even the television was badly hampered, so badly it could show but a few hundred feet ahead as they followed the leading ship closely. Anto Rayl was silent, intently watching the screen.

———◈———

The destroyer ahead was making straight for the largest of the near-by islands. And, as they neared it, a peninsula a quarter of a mile long slid silently out to sea and sank beneath the waves. A great metal-lined bore was revealed, and instantly the destroyer dropped into it. The *Sunbeam* was directly behind. That bore was an oval cylinder, five hundred feet wide, and two hundred long, and extending down beyond sight, curving into the bowels of the planet.

The lighted bore was suddenly darkened by the settling of the great rocky lid back in place.

The tunnel had straightened out. Now, suddenly, they came upon a great factory, a huge, brightly lighted underground workshop. Gigantic forms were in construction off across the big, pillared cavern.

"This is San-toa," said Anto at that moment. "We wish to show you our ships. You have shown us yours—"

Aarn laughed good-naturedly. "Haven't shown you anything," he replied.

Anto looked down at the shorter man in surprise. "Nothing?" he asked in surprise. "But surely we have seen the machinery?"

"You could not duplicate it. It is hidden within itself. But I will show you things you must make. Those two new battleships—have them tear out the accumulators you have. I will give them a better kind. The type you are using we have had on Earth for many years, and this type is far better. Further, I must have a power ship built—"

Aarn Munro talked rapidly. He talked, in the end, to a hundred scientists of this world, Magya, and showed them a thousand things. And he gave them specifications. Then he talked to the space-force staff and showed them a greater source of power lay in the sun.

"To fight successfully, you need power. I will give you three things that can be installed in all your battleships; the accumulators, the so-called aggie coils, the magnetic atmosphere which renders the Shal torpedoes useless and stops the lightning balls, and the transpon beam, which will cut holes in battleships. To do this, the battleships must have a greater power supply. A fourth thing I may be able to install, an automatic acceleration neutralizer that will release your men of the strain of motion.

"The power supply will be obtained in this way: A series of four mother ships, with their thin walls, their huge accumulator volume, must be stripped at once, and the new type accumulator put in, and with it such apparatus as I shall show you. These ships will make the trip to the sun, faster than light, collect the needed energy, and return loaded. They can charge four battleships, eight heavy cruisers, or twelve light cruisers. That must be done for victory!"

CHAPTER IX

"WE HAVE," SAID CARLISLE with annoyance, "been here for forty-seven of their long days, and we seem to have gotten nowhere. The Tefflans have, on the other hand, conducted a successful raid in which three heavy cruisers and a warship were destroyed with the loss of two light cruisers, and a damaged battleship."

Spencer smiled wanly. "Brother Trolley Car, what you need is work. You've been wandering around San Toa here like a lost soul and doing nothing."

"What could I do?" demanded Carlisle angrily. "That's what gets me. I'm not used to loafing. I couldn't even help particularly when you ripped the old *Sunbeam* to pieces and made her over. The only thing that's left that I know anything about is the kitchen and the air apparatus. You tore out the lab, the calculating room, the lounge, most of the quarters, and loaded in more accumulator coils. Then you crowded so darned much junk in that power room I don't know what all is there. I know you have a lightning apparatus—but what else have you?"

Aarn smiled smugly. "Much the same in the other three fields. Ball lightning is an electric field of one sign that is self-maintaining because its intensity is so great it simply wraps itself into a pocket in space. As soon as any great intensity of another field enters it, it unwraps—and then look out.

"The ball lightning has one difficulty; it always goes bang at the surface of the thing it touches. So I tried ball-magnetic field. We got that. That has the advantage of—well, look. I even made a riflelike model for the spy ships to carry."

Aarn's "riflelike" model must have weighed one hundred and fifty pounds, but the Jovian handled it with ease. He led Carlisle out of their quarters, down through the laboratory that had been taken from the *Sunbeam* and set up in one of the bright-lighted chambers the Magyans had hewn in the solid rock of the planet with the aid of the wonderful Shal torpedoes.

At the far end of the laboratory were several heavy sheets of armor plate, steel twelve inches thick, so heavy that they were more nearly described as blocks than as sheets. Yet the great battleships carried this plate as light inner-hull armor, while blocks four feet thick made the outer hull.

"Now remember: This fires a magnetic-ball field. It will proceed to set itself inside the magnetic material, and then release its energy. An electric-ball field tends to spread itself on the surface and release. A gravitational field is even better, since it seeks the center of gravity of the body and then releases. But a little spy ship is so light it has no effective center of gravity of its own. The battleships and cruisers are the fellows those will go after."

Aarn raised the strangely shaped weapon and pressed the trigger release. There was a thud somewhere inside, then a steady stream of strangely glowing orange balls shot out of the muzzle and curved gently to one side as they sped across the room. They struck the heavy metal, though, because they jerked sharply out of their course toward it. The first struck and was buried in the metal.

Instantly an explosion occurred inside the metal that made a three-inch blister on the surface. The next was a little to one side and arrived perhaps a hundredth of a second later. A third followed, and a fourth. The result of several hundred of these ball fields was a suddenly opening cleft of white-hot iron that tore the heavy armor in two instantly.

"That," explained Aarn, "is the general idea."

"Will it do the same on the heavy stuff the battleships carry?" asked Carlisle.

"Well—not quite so well. The big ships carry such thick armor it will dissipate the energy almost as fast as we can get it there, with the result that the thing has to eat its way gradually through, and can't, because the ship moves. I'll admit the Shal torpedoes have their points. We're improving those, by the way, by putting magnetic grips on them that will pull them on as long as there's anything stopping them."

"Hm-m-m—I have an idea. I wonder if there are any chemists around here," said Carlisle softly. "I'm going to have a talk with Mayno Shar."

Carlisle wandered off in a sudden dense fog of thought. Spencer stared after him in amazement, and a broad grin spread across Aarn's face.

"Well, and that's that," said Spencer.

"He's got an idea, and when he gets one that hard, one's all he can handle." Munro grinned. "I'd like to know what it is, though."

They learned a few hours later, when Carlisle and Mayno Shar came back together, talking earnestly. They wanted aluminum. And they wanted iron oxide, and magnesium, and a magnetic-field-ball device.

Aarn had to help them, but he was as interested as they, by the thing they turned out finally—a round bomb of thick graphite, filled with a charge of iron oxide and aluminum powder, with a detonator attachment, and a projector that would project it by means of a spring catapult. Compressed air would have had less tendency to injure the bomb, but the gas would be difficult to obtain and require heavy equipment to carry it in space.

They tried the finished bomb, some four feet in diameter, on an old piece of battleship-armor plate the next day. From a projector tube placed on the side of a destroyer, the bomb was held.

The physical mechanism functioned perfectly. Though the armor plate was being jerked about by another destroyer, and though equipped with even a repulsing space disk, the bomb found its hold and clung.

For ten seconds nothing happened. Then a red light suddenly glowed over the bomb, it turned white—and simultaneously a terrible pencil of blinding, blue-white radiance sputtered out of a one-inch hole in the side of the bomb that touched the plate of metal.

That one-inch stream fused the metal as suddenly as a stream of boiling water would fuse a cake of ice. It ate holes in the armor as it slowly spun around, and within one minute the terrible, blinding stream of white-hot, boiling iron and aluminum shot through the armor and on into space, squirting out under the pressure of the vaporous iron inside the now white-hot graphite bomb.

No other substance known could have resisted the terrific heat, and, though mechanically weak, graphite had served.

Had that armor plate been part of a vessel, a gaping hole would have been cut, through which the air would have escaped. Then that incredibly fierce flame of melted, boiling iron would have squirted over whatsoever might lie behind.

"I thought of that," said Carlisle with satisfaction, "because of an experiment I once saw as a demonstration of thermite. The lecturer had a crucible of iron with the thermite mixture suspended over a vertical series of ten other iron crucibles, and finally a pan of sand. He started the thermite, and a drop of that incredibly hot iron fused its way through the bottom of the first crucible, and then *plink-plink-plink-plink-plink*—right through every single one of those other iron crucibles, and ended up by fusing some of that sand to glass.

"You know, it is almost unthinkable—the effect of having a real quantity of matter at a temperature like that."

"It is," admitted Aarn. "I never really respected the power of chemistry so much. That's a heat ray for sure. Physics couldn't make one, but when you turn your little hose loose and—"

"I wonder," suggested Spencer, "if we couldn't do just that—use a hose?"

"No," replied Aarn quickly. "The white-hot stuff would cool too quickly—cool before it reached its target."

"No," said Carlisle simultaneously, "because the graphite would evaporate and burn somewhat with each firing. The crucible would have to be replaced, and you couldn't make anything to hold the holder. The crucible gets so hot you couldn't hold it, remember."

"I want to ride in that new battleship when they finish it," said Spencer.

"It's a beautiful thing," agreed Aarn, "but remember that nothing is absolutely immune to attack. It's conceivable that the Tefflans might develop some new weapon that would destroy it instantly. That thermite trick would certainly make it look sick if it ever got through the magnetic atmosphere."

"But with the things it's got—the gravity-field ball, magnetic-field balls, besides electric, the magnetic atmosphere, that interference device to stop the radio-frequency induction, the aggie coils for power—even momentum wave drive, and the faster-than-light escape, if necessary. You couldn't touch it!" Spencer scoffed.

"No, listen: Nothing man ever made was beyond man's power of destruction," snapped Aarn. "I could destroy that battleship with the little *Sunbeam*. Suppose I attached about fifty of those thermite leeches of Carlisle's. You couldn't escape them by running away, because they'd just dig in their magnetic toes and hang on.

"Add that I smashed an unexpected transpon beam loaded with everything those big aggie banks we now carry could give, and headed it straight for their own main aggie-coil bank. I'd have them underpowered in a fraction of a second. Their faster-than-light escape wouldn't work, their armor would be full of holes, and the ship full of white-hot iron spray.

"A few gravity-ball fields would settle down comfortably somewhere in the neighborhood of the main antigravity coils and blow them to kingdom come. The point being that I could, with a sudden attack of unexpected ferocity, cripple the thing so it couldn't run before it could get started. Then everything else in sight could pile on—and good-by Ma-jhay-anhy!"

"But the Tefflans have no *Sunbeam*," protested Carlisle.

"They haven't been idle—and they know that they're in for some new kind of trouble," replied Spencer. "I see Aarn's point."

———◇———

"What are the plans of the Magyans in regard to further battles?" asked Carlisle.

"Anto Rayl said—that they wanted to finish another squadron of the aggie-supply ships and set up heavier defenses on the four moons here. Then they plan to launch a grand attack on Teff-el and simply wipe it out. The present plan, for one thing, involves the use of Teff-el's moon, Teff-ran. Teff-el has only one moon, and it's about three hundred miles in diameter. They plan to capture it—and use it for ammunition to destroy Teff-el!"

"Sweet wavering worlds! How could they?" gasped Carlisle.

"Not impossible now," Aarn said earnestly and eagerly. "They thought of using antigravity coils and freeing it of Teff-el's attraction; but I convinced them that they'd be wasting a lot of power loosening Anrel's greater attraction, so they simply plan to attach a huge system of momentum-wave engines and drive straight into the planet with all the energy they possibly can. That's one reason for the extra fleet of supply ships. Those aggie ships will be regular mobile aggie coils, and not much more. About one million tons of aggie coil."

The soft musical hum of the door annunciator sounded, and presently Aarn returned with Anto Rayl in tow—and highly excited.

"A scout ship just came back—they've been circling Teff-el for the last twenty days at a speed so great that no photographic plate could catch them, and painted so black no eye could see them—and the men report a huge war formation is leaving. That means an attack in full force."

"That means something else—they've got something distinctly new to fight with, and they hope they can do so much damage to you right now that you won't be able to use the things that the *Sunbeam* had. They know that you have the secrets we had, and they know that small ship was invulnerable to the attacks of their largest and heaviest. If they are picking a fight now, that means something new and deadly. Send one of the new destroyers out to attack, and have a fleet of the new scouts near by to watch. We'll go, and you can meet us at the *Sunbeam*, Anto Rayl."

"That is the plan," said Anto Rayl, smoothly, "formulated by the High Command."

Anto laughed slightly, bitterly, and went on: "Do not think we have been fighting these Tefflans for centuries without learning their every thought. We are worried, I may say, for they know ours."

CHAPTER X

THE GUARD FLEET STATIONED near Magya itself had dropped far behind now, and the formation of the fleet was perfect as it swept up and on into space. A disk of scout ships was flung wide ahead, with the occasional new scout ships of the type capable of faster-than-light speeds scattered as messengers.

Behind this warning disk, ten thousand miles behind, came the fleet, a huge sphere of restlessly weaving destroyers, an inner sphere of cruisers, both light and heavy, and then the solid might of the great battleships.

In the forefront of the battleships was the *Sunbeam*, her occupants watching interestedly the views on the television, relayed from the leading destroyer. A tiny cloud of dust in space far ahead represented the attacking Tefflan fleet, hurling itself forward to the battle eagerly. Telescopes were trained on them from the scout ships ahead, and suddenly half a dozen scout ships vanished from their places, to appear beside the battleships of the Magyans.

Despite all rules of space warfare, the Tefflans were sending their heaviest battleships ahead, in the lead, with the heavy cruisers re-enforcing them. There were ten of the heaviest ships, and all very evidently new. And the cruisers were all equipped with new apparatus, something the trained eyes of the Magyans had detected instantly.

Two great Magyan battleships suddenly leaped forward, speeded, and vanished in speed greater than light. They were to be sacrifice ships if necessary, but those two giant ships out of Magya's active fleet of thirty-six were deadly machines.

Their own fleet dropped swiftly behind and then vanished to them, while the fleet ahead shifted and shimmered in the strange effects of their speed. They swooped nearer, then, suddenly, were almost among the Tefflan ships—and appeared. The Tefflans had had no warning, for none could race through space faster than light, and the warning the Magyans might have given trailed somewhere behind.

For thirty seconds the Magyan battleships operated with every piece of offensive apparatus they possessed. A thousand giant thermite bombs spattered out of each, to seek and hold a place on some enemy ship. Thousands of terrific magnetic balls shot forth, to bury their fangs in the armor of some cruisers, and rip a great gap in it; to heat the armor of some battleship yellow, hot, and soft. Sudden terrific explosions must have echoed deep within cruiser and battleship as gravity-field balls sank, reached the center, and blasted their energy in the heart of the ship.

And each great battleship was slicing about with six transpon beams, not such as that the *Sunbeam* had used, but run by far vaster power coils. They cut through a cruiser's armor instantly and sliced it cleanly in two. They burned and sputtered at a mighty battleship's armor, and cut and bored through to the heart of the ship. Shal torpedoes lurched and ground and shuddered their way into weakened armor, and great white-hot holes appeared where thermite sprays ate their way through.

So sudden and terrific was the attack that the cruiser force was nigh destroyed before any realization of the presence of an enemy was possible.

Destroyed—but not destroyed. For though the cruisers were sliced by the transpon beams, their armor pierced by thermite and magnetic bombs, their hearts blasted by gravity-energy bombs, they were carefully designed to withstand and operate under any conceivable punishment, and the Tefflans had designed well.

The ten great battleships were crippled, their walls punctured by the thermite, twisted and softened by magnetic bombs, their deepest center torn and blasted by gravity bombs, but their engines might be wrecked and leave them by far the greater part of their energy—the wide-scattered accumulators.

Shells were flying from the battleships and the cruisers, torpedoes—but they turned aside and exploded far from the Magyan ships. Great induction beams snapped out—and died a flaming death on the screens of interference that Magyan ships had been equipped with for fifty millia.

Then every man in the fore part on the great Magyan battleship *Hantu Toa* stiffened suddenly at his post, and writhed and twisted in sudden grating, grinding agony, his nerves shivered and shuddered, his uncontrollable muscles jerked and snapped about, his eyes grew dim, and his hearing ceased. Meaningless shouts of uncontrolled sound burst from them, and they toppled—dead.

Slowly, inexorably, the thing crept backward—and another wave started at the stern and worked forward. A mad hand touched something—the great mass of steel hurtled forward at thousands of miles a second, suddenly driven into another space, and swiftly gaining velocity. It tangled, somehow, with the electric fields in the accumulators of a Tefflan ship, and both vanished in an intolerable blaze of energy.

The *Anlan Toa* suddenly turned and vanished in speed greater than light. The unknown secret was known. For the fore part of the *Anlan Toa* had been touched, and men had jerked and bellowed and died. The Magyan fleet had halted and hung motionless now, waiting. Swiftly a dozen scientists entered the *Anlan Toa* and looked. They had the answer in seconds. A few glances—

"Coagulated," said Carlisle as he saw the tissue of the dead men.

"And I know how. Super-sonic waves," Aarn put in softly. "They induce them somehow in our ships. How in—got it, I think. Make us do it. It's the radio-frequency induction beam heterodyning our own defense interference, somehow, into supersonics."

"Then if we turned off our own interference that would prevent these deaths?" asked a Magyan somewhat doubtfully.

"I think so. Send a destroyer—let them try that. One of the new ones, lest torpedoes or other weapons destroy it," suggested Aarn eagerly.

A destroyer vanished as it shot ahead, a destroyer equipped with momentum-wave drive, magnetic atmosphere, the transpon beams, and powered by aggie coils.

They watched it by television screens relayed from tiny spy ships up there on the front. They saw the destroyer appear suddenly, spray a collection of the deadly thermite bombs that clung and burned and ate. Magnetic-ball fields, gravitational-ball fields shot out. Torpedoes. A transpon beam that sputtered through the armor of half a cruiser that was as active as ever the whole had been.

For seconds the destroyer continued operating, a sputtering transpon beam driving its white-hot needle to the heart of a great battleship now, slicing through accumulator banks. The battleship suddenly began to blossom with blue-white spots of eating thermite spray. The deadly stuff was spewing out in a dozen two-inch streams. The destroyer released a new flock of torpedoes—

And its outlines softened gradually, and it spread, as though the disintegration process of time, of a billion billion years, had been encompassed in a dozen seconds. Then it suddenly puffed gigantic, a dust cloud, through which still burning lights showed, but vanished suddenly, with sudden flaming, sputtering transpon beams that fought and stabbed and blew up huge stores of aggie energy.

The little spy ship that bore the televisor suddenly reeled and quivered under the released field impulses.

But the destroyer was gone.

The Magyan turned to Munro, his face white.

Munro was staring ahead in horror, in terrified bewilderment. "Disintegration—they disintegrated it!" he gasped. Slowly he passed his hand across his eyes, and a look of deep puzzlement came. "But—they could not do that. It's—it's impossible!"

"They did it!" snapped the Magyan.

"They didn't. They only seem to have," replied Aarn half consciously. He was thinking: "We're going aboard the *Sunbeam*."

The solarites went back to their ship. And Aarn was silent as he looked ahead.

"I think—I know—"

His fingers flew as he let up a dozen controls. Then he pressed one. The fleet around them vanished. They were diving headlong through the mass of broken and damaged Tefflan ships. On—on—to the main mass of the great battle fleet.

In the exact center of the battle fleet Aarn stopped. "We are," he said, "invisible. I have left a small hole so that the television eyes can see. They know we are here and presently will, I suspect, be doing something about it.

"I'm going to open up this shell of mine—no; I won't have to—yes; I will. I'll open up, and send them a flaming invitation to battle in the form of all our thermite bombs, and our best wishes wrapped up in ball-gravity fields. Carlisle, you handle the thermite. I'll handle the ship. Spencer, take the gravity."

They saw little change, but at Aarn's signal, they began to work. It was rapid, for the *Sunbeam* spun quickly on her axis. Aarn had added the transpon beam, and cut a terrible swath of white-hot destruction through half a dozen destroyers that had come in to the battleship squadron to see what was the cause of the terrific field disturbances.

"One"—said Aarn—"you have five—three—four—gone. The field's shut. Watch!"

———◆———

The thermite bombs were seeking anchorage. The gravity bombs found victim after victim, a flash of lurid light, a few score exploding ports, and a sudden wild movement of the struck ship as the lights going out momentarily told of that.

The thermite bombs took hold. A score of them had been released from the twin tubes, and now a score of ships felt the blistering two-inch stream of white-hot iron.

The television apparatus abruptly went dead. There was a tinkling and whistling—and then Aarn grinned as it stopped.

"I thought that would stop it."

In answer to Aarn's contented expression, there was a sudden terrific scream of tortured metal, a flash of terrific light from somewhere behind them, then the clang of automatic doors shutting. Aarn blanched, and there was the whine and thump of heavy transpon beams in action. He ran silently for several seconds, then shutters moved from the window. They were in empty space.

"I neglected to consider these things. That explosion that seems to have dented in the rear portion of our hull was caused by one of those ball-lightning discharges. It simply was sucked into the field that stopped the light, and that field was so tight, the ball lightning touched our shell. Now, I can't make an invisibility device work, because they can find it.

"That death ray killed off the crew of those ships—that's heterodyne with the radio-frequency beam. They have something else—something carrying millions of horse power. Must have some wonderful apparatus to do it. It's—a fatigue ray. It does exactly what those Shal torpedoes do, only does it along a beam. It doesn't break by its energy. It doesn't fuse. It simply crumbles things. I got an analysis on it from those controls I set up.

"They had it arranged for the best values on iron and steel. We have beryllo-aluminum walls largely. The thing didn't get that right off. You see steel is made up largely of crystals, and while a pretty good conductor, those crystals can have a distinct difference of potential across their faces. And there is a sort of insulation between each.

"They have a radio-frequency beam of some sort that simply starts pounding the individual crystals of steel, and all those that happen to lie on just about the right frequency start vibrating in tune—and all of a sudden they break and turn to the finest sort of liquid dust. The strength goes out of the stuff and leaves the most useless sort of granular, rotten metal. Fatigue. Too much pounding. They pound it a couple of million times a second and give it a million years' natural fatigue in a second.

"Now here's the pleasant situation. If we keep up the radio-frequency interference screen, the disintegrating beam is stopped. If we do keep it up, though, they start their heterodyning stunt, which is probably done with the same beam, and kill all the men. If we take it down to save the men—they crumble the ship."

"Then what can we do, Aarn?" demanded Anto Rayl.

"Fight!" replied Aarn grimly. "It's a terrible blow to learn this—but think also that they are suffering, because they thought to disintegrate your ships safely from a distance. They won't. That's your consolation."

Anto Rayl made a wry mouth. "It is sour consolation."

The television screen came back to life as Martin and Canning finished their repairs. Canning reported that the damage caused by the explosion amounted to seven destroyed aggie coils, and three plates fused away. No great damage had been done, really, but it might have finished the trip.

"We will tell your people," said Aarn, as the Magyan fleet suddenly appeared on the television screen, "and they must fight. That is all I can offer now. Their best method will be to release their bombs, far, wide, and handsome, in the knowledge that no bombs can endanger their own ships, while every bomb that wanders loose is an additional danger to every Tefflan ship. Tell them, too, to try using the screen, and dropping it rapidly—alternating, say, anywhere from one to ten times a second, and hope for a good effect."

The battleships were well behind now, as the fleets neared each other, and at the suggestion of a Magyan scientist, the entire fleet of momentum drive equipped ships suddenly acquired the greatest possible momentum, released all the bombs available, then fell back with the rest of the fleet. More bombs were acquired from the supply ships, as the Tefflan fleet maneuvered more slowly into position.

The bombs struck without warning. They had been moving at terrific speed, and they swept in, in a solid front. At a thousand miles they began to illuminate Tefflan hulls, splotches of blinding radiation.

The great battleships of the Tefflan fleet were almost indestructible, but before the terrible lashing attack of thousands of thermite bombs, the searing flame of the transpon beams, and the crippling attack of the gravity bombs, even the greatest might be beaten down.

The cruisers, the destroyers, and the lighter craft vanished under the attack of swift-darting spy ships and scouts. Here, for the first time, the scout ship became a prime instrument of war, for, loaded with aggie coils, and equipped with the invisible transpon beams, they were so tiny as they darted about, without lights and black in black space, that they could actually wander in among the cruisers and destroyers of the enemy, and with their deadly transpon beams, they were capable of ripping a destroyer open.

The Tefflan destroyers carried disintegrating, or fatigue-ray apparatus, but not powerful enough to operate against anything larger than a scout ship, and the scout ships were far speedier, far harder to find. The Tefflan destroyers retired in haste, and were wiped out completely by scout ships they could not locate.

Their own scout and spy ships were destroyed utterly by the little two-man spy ships of the Magyan forces. Equipped with aggie coils and momentum drive, the one thousand new spy ships could maneuver far more swiftly. The torpedoes and shells of the enemy were useless, as the magnetic atmosphere stopped them, and the scout ships of Tefflan carried no death ray or fatigue ray.

The battle was fought at long range, by mutual consent. Tefflan lost her destroyers, her spy and scout ships. What destroyers were not accounted for by the hundreds of thermite bombs, or by a well-placed gravity or magnetic bomb, or ripped open by a transpon beam, escaped under the sacrificial cloud of scout and spy ships.

But the great cruisers, and even the light cruisers, were proof against the scout ships, and the battleships were not even annoyed by them. The light cruisers made it their duty to seek out and destroy the somewhat dangerous scout ships. Their armor would glow and sputter under the combined attack of four or five transpon beams, a cloud of gas would be released to make the beam visible, and then a fatigue ray would shoot back along it.

The main battle, though, was between the battleships of each side, for Magyan battleships could stand a short exposure to the fatigue ray. No damage was done until the actual weakening suddenly and spontaneously occurred. It was a process of building up molecular-crystal vibrations till the crystals finally snapped, and until that point was reached there was no damage. Then, there was all damage.

The enormous mass of a battleship wall absorbed a tremendous amount of energy, and only when several beams got in perfect phase was the result quick.

Too, by using the screen for a brief part of a second, the interruption, coming once every hundredth of a second, was able to weaken the effect, as the vibrations damped out in the protected period, and the exposure meant only a mild, steady torture to the men within the ship.

<hr />

Thirty great battleships formed the front, against twenty-nine whole Tefflan battleships, but there were no less than eleven half ships in action, and each of these was fully half as deadly as a full battleship.

The Tefflan beams reached out—but weakened by distance. Similarly, the deadly transpon beams were weakened in distance. But the transpon beams could heat the great battleships slowly, if they held, and that meant unbearable conditions within. The trouble lay in the fact that the men aboard the Magyan ships were tortured with jerking muscles, as the supersonic waves struck them, just mildly, but enough to make their control poor, their aim bad.

The *Sunbeam* hung far back. She had no walls thick and strong enough to withstand even a momentary attack of the beam if applied on the right frequency. Instead, she was occupying herself in sending bombs.

"I think," said Aarn softly, "this battle will go to Magya. I think it is certain to. It would have gone to Tefflan, but the destroyers and cruisers of each fleet are almost worthless, and the Tefflan commanders realize that the battleships could never pass the heavy defenses on the four moons and on Magya itself. And the cruisers can't help now."

"What good are these bombs doing?" asked Spencer in exasperation. "Can't we make another flying attack in there and get out before they spot us?"

"They've spotted us right now. They probably know just where we are, and the instant we disappeared, their observers would be watching for us back among 'em. They'd have us floating in a sea of electric flame before we stopped moving," Munro said precisely.

"Further, these bombs are doing a lot of good. They are disconcerting. The Tefflans' generals and scientists may have figured out how it is done, but that's less comfort to them than the knowledge of the general idea of that death ray to us. We can do something about that, but they can't stop these things. And these have no distance limit.

"The center of every single one of those battleships and cruisers up there is an exploding, white-hot danger point. Not one of those ships has any heart left. The engine room is gone, and, probably, half the reserve apparatus, the commanding officer, and the main controls. The big thing is—those ships have no source of power."

"Say, if those gentle little toys have no source of power," Carlisle said bitterly, "I'd like to see one *with* a source of power."

"They are drawing on accumulated power. Heck of a difference!" said Munro. "The accumulators are exhaustible. If the thing keeps up indefinitely, they'll be sunk, because they can't get home without power, and— Sweet stellar spectra! That's a thought!"

Aarn turned the *Sunbeam* suddenly, applied all his power, and headed for Magya. They leaped to the planet faster than light. In swift syllables he explained to Anto Rayl, and when they slowed to less than the speed of light over San Toa, Anto signalled for the opening of the great gateway.

Again the clouding steam, and again they sank into the island. With familiarity, Aarn hurled the *Sunbeam* at a reckless pace through the tunnel and into the hangar which was hers. He was out of the ship and into his laboratory in great leaping bounces, the bounces of a Jovian on a lighter world, and in a hurry.

Spencer was after him, calling Canning to accompany him. Aarn was already at work on the calculating machine, and with a great loose-leaf notebook filled with fine-lettered data. Minutes sped by into hours as Aarn labored.

Information was brought in from the battle front. Conditions remained almost the same now, balanced, though one of the Magyan battleships had failed in her fore quarters and collapsed utterly. She was turned about now and still functioning, while most of the light cruisers of the Tefflan forces had left the front and retired far behind the lines, out of range of the aiming powers of the various bombs. The scout ships were still tearing at them, however.

And one Tefflan battleship half was out of action and limping home.

<hr>

Two hours passed, and at last Aarn had what he wanted. In half an hour he had designed a mechanism to do the work. In an hour more Canning had turned it into three different types of patterns.

Scout ships came in from the fleet some three hours later to pick up newly made apparatus. The things were crude—simple.

The messages that had come to Magya had been equaled in number by the messages going out. And some of those had gone from the great headquarters on Magya. The result had been a steady retreat, the sacrifice of two old-type destroyers, with radio control operated over miles-long cables. Tefflan seemed to be winning. Six great battleships had fallen back and were evidently undergoing repair, the supply ships clustering near them.

Tefflan ships advanced. But presently, about the time the scout ships began racing out to the fleet with the new apparatus, they became worried and started retreating rapidly themselves.

Magya followed just as rapidly, at a distance. Tefflan ships retreated more rapidly, and some of the cruisers which had retired came up and battled bravely. But uselessly, for they were drowned in great transpon beams, as one huge battleship after another leaped close and retired before seriously weakened.

The battleships of Tefflan were in frank retreat, but the Magyans held on like leeches, attacking vigorously, and the Tefflans realized in dismay that their opponents would not leave them. In haste, the Tefflans raced for the protection of the great defenses on the planet, the one moon of Teff-el, and the ten orbital forts they had set up.

And one by one the great Magyan battleships started their new apparatus as it was installed. Crude—not very effective—but the momentum-wave field was distorted and twisted, till it gripped the Tefflan ships. Like a gigantic hand, it clutched them and slowed them. The six battleships that had fallen behind came up now, nearer than before, then held back also.

Frantically the Tefflan commanders turned their waning power into the drive, while cruisers attacked desperately to free the greater ships. Grimly, the Magyan battle fleet held on and rained terrific magnetic-field bombs on the cruisers, that warped and twisted and fused their frames and their armor, and the Shal torpedoes ate their way in.

There were no more thermite bombs, but the gravity bombs were being supplied now largely from the six ships which had retired to the supply ships and had all their power coils recharged. The gravitational balls were wasting their energy in a compartment they had blasted to gas and molten waste.

The accumulators which had been centered here were gone, along with the engines. The Tefflan captains saw their power declining—the last dregs of energy slipping away.

Huge fatigue rays drove at the now-close Magyan ships, and the armor and frames began to crumble slowly—slowly. The ships fell back abruptly. Those ships were deserted, too weak now, and radio-controlled. Their momentum drives pulled back, and the Tefflan ships pulled on. Their beams were wasted once more in disintegrating the huge masses of those four old hulks.

After that, they had no hope. Their power was so far gone, to attempt to destroy more ships meant complete loss of the entire fleet. The Magyan ships closed in. Heavy cruisers of the Magyan fleet closed in—

Bright transpon beams sectioned the Tefflan hulks neatly and with dispatch a few thousand miles beyond the ultimate range of the orbital forts and the planetary defense beams. The battleships were sectioned, and each ship of the Magyan fleet took a piece in tow according to its power.

The cruisers were sectioned where they had been destroyed further in space, and the five-hundred-million-mile trip back to Magya begun.

Teff-el, was, for the first time in centuries, totally without a battle fleet, and yet the Magyan ships did not dare to approach. For those orbital forts were as invulnerable to a battleship as a battleship might be to a one-man spy ship without weapons.

And, further, Magya received back, of its thirty-six brave battleships, seventeen. A battle between battleships of space is not like a sea battle, for the battleship of space never sinks, and every portion is capable of fighting until every man within is killed; a battle between space battleships is to the death of every individual. When space battleships were destroyed, they were annihilated completely. Only the millions of tons of fined steel that the Magyans were towing back remained.

There was no hope of learning the secret of the death beams and the fatigue ray, for the apparatus had been fused completely by a built-in accumulator. A touch of an emergency button, the release of all air pressure on a special valve—and the apparatus was reduced to scrap.

So, though Tefflan contributed millions of tons of steel to the new battle fleet, they contributed no knowledge.

CHAPTER XI

AARN WAS WORRIED AS he rejoined his friends after the conference.

Spencer looked at him questioningly. "Couldn't make anything out of the wreckage?"

"No," replied Aarn; "but that's not what's worrying me. That's a minor point. We don't need that, with the latest plan. I suggested it, and I got us into trouble. Quite rightly, and with every reason, the Magyans are wild for it. They gave a great whoop of joy, and fell on my weakened frame from all sides, but—"

"What," asked Spencer, annoyed, "caused this demonstration of joy? What was the inspiration?"

"Eh—oh! The moon ship idea. You know—need something heavier to stand up against that new beam. Simple idea—fairly obvious, isn't it?"

"Again, nit-wit, what? I can't get what you mean by a 'moon ship'; they've had ships to go to moons and beyond for millia on millia."

"Oh, I mean the whole moon. They have four. They want to use two in the plan—Ma-ran and Ma-kanee. That's numbers one and four. The inner moon is about one hundred miles in diameter, you know, and somebody figured it would be a grand thing because nobody could make a device powerful enough to start disintegration waves in that, and so it would be safe to use it as a fort as before. And then I asked why not use it to attack, and they thought it was a good—"

"Well, I'll be a square circle! Sweet swinging satellites! Break it loose and use it for a battleship—and what a battleship! No armor, but too big to hurt—" Spencer stared in ecstasy. "Good lord—a whole moon for a battle-ship, charging across space for five hundred million miles!"

"Oh, not quite a battleship—just a sort of map." Munro grinned. "You see, the Tefflan orbital forts and Teff-el's moon, Teff-ran, are all so deadly they can't bring their battleships in close. But Teff-ran, of course, has no driving mechanism, and the orbital forts have just enough driving mechanism to keep their orbits stable and regular. Everything else is fighting apparatus.

"So they thought they'd use a Shal torpedo device to run a tunnel clear to the center, set up a huge driving apparatus of the momentum drive type—and—just go down and circulate around Teff-el. They could simply ruin all those orbital forts—what it would do to the forts would be final.

"Then the men aboard would set the drive full blast, escape in a scout ship, and let the whole thing ride straight at Teff-ran. Teff-ran is bigger—considerably—but with Ma-ran traveling about fifty miles a second and the mass of quintillions of tons—that will be all there is to that.

"Meanwhile, trailing behind, and falling all the way in a straight line toward Anrel's mighty sphere, will be the seven-hundred-mile-diameter Ma-kanee. It will be aimed straight at Teff-el—"

"And that will end Magya's worries for once and for all," finished Spencer. "If they can do it. Can they?"

"That alone wouldn't end their worries," replied the physicist, "because they might be able to escape by shiploads, you know, and start another colony. But, in the meantime, a ring of battleships and scout ships will surround the planet and put a stop to that. These Magyans mean business. They don't intend to have Tefflans attacking humans any more. They did that once, you know—we did? Anyway, Earth doesn't have them any more. These fellows are thorough—"

He paused with a grim little gesture of finality. "They can do it with time. They intend to build a fleet of no less than fifty supply ships, and keep up a constant stream of charged coils to the planet from Anrel. Also send a sunbeam all the way to Anrel. With a giant sun like that behind them, it's no question of power enough. The momentum-wave device means that the question of drive is settled. They have only the physical problem of manufacturing coils enough to store the power.

"They plan to accelerate the moons till they simply widen their orbits to freedom. That will prevent any sudden shifting of tidal effects on Magya. They feel that no harm will result, but the astronomers and mathematicians are at work calculating.

"I feel confident that, with time, they can do it. They have an enormous advantage in that supply of steel they took from Tefflan. Teff-el must be hard put right now to mine an entirely new supply of metal, besides the problem of labor. And their work is going to be speeded to the utmost."

"Why worry? Just use that traveling moon to perambulate through a few battleships, too." Carlisle laughed.

Spencer looked pained beyond words. "Go get a whale to slap mosquitoes with. Use an elephant to crush little brown fleas. Get a transpon beam to shoot down butterflies. With the difference that the battleships would simply dodge, and come around behind, land on your perambulating world, and start digging their way inside. It's bad enough using it on those huge forts; they really intend to use it on the fortified moon there. And, I suspect, on Teff-el itself. Right?"

Aarn nodded. "They'll calculate a course of impact that will carry the broken masses straight down to Teff-el. That alone will cause damage enough.

"The danger of waiting is that they will build up a fleet of speedy ships, well equipped with death beams and disintegrators, realizing that the warfare is now reduced to two types—a light, swift, almost invisible scout-ship type, and the great behemoth battleships. They haven't the time or the metal for the battleships. But they may build the light fellows, and then they could escape.

"The next time they'll have ships that can fight our scouts and spies more effectively. Also, next time they are going to have a nice, empty, insulated cylinder in the exact center of their ships, so that our gravity bombs can explode in peace—and harmlessness. They may not know how it's done, but they learned quick enough what was happening, you can bet.

"But I haven't yet told you what's been worrying me. The plans are good. But they mean the one-hundred-and-one percent annihilation of Teff-el. They mean destruction more thorough, more complete and final, than anything you can imagine. That planet will be just a mass of drifting asteroids.

"And somewhere, on some one of the countless thousands of asteroids, buried in a terrible, inextricable mess of incalculable orbits, will float serenely a bit of planet with eleven thick plates of gleaming silvery metal engraved with age-old characters, eleven plates of osmiridio-platinum alloy that would endure for ages, carrying the data that would get us back where we came from—"

"And no one in the universe or the universes could ever find them again."

Spencer and Carlisle were stricken suddenly silent.

"What'll we do?" gasped Carlisle at length.

"Exactly!" Aarn nodded. "What'll we do? Santin Rao has ordered immediate work on the great project, and they calculate that not more than eighty days will be needed to complete it. Somehow, within those eighty days, we must recover those eleven plates of osmiridio-platinum. Otherwise we spend the rest of our natural existences here. Not that it's unpleasant—but it isn't home. I could get that data—with thirty years' work and calculation. These fellows have never attempted to get it. They weren't interested. Too much else on hand."

"Have you any idea where, on Teff-el, they are?" asked Spencer.

"None. But at my plea, Santin Rao is going to have every attempt possible made to find them. And I'm going to make some little things—they may help."

"What?" asked Spencer eagerly.

"Eh—a little thing—I don't know if it will work, or if we can make it or—" Aarn paused.

"Oh, shut up! Another one of your secrets. All right—take it away—and listen to this one: Carlisle, here, tells me he's got an idea from something you said about physics, and some studying he's been doing, that may help us a lot if we ever have to raid Teff-el."

"I hope so. We'll need more than help; we'll need a miracle to recover those tablets. With modern spacial warfare, a fight over the city or building where those plates are means the destruction of everything within a million miles of it. That means that somehow we have to get those plates secretly. That's the devil of it."

"Sweet chance of slipping by all those guards the Tefflans have. Spy ships. Orbital forts. Telescopes. Probably some form of detector device."

"Yes—the Magyans have the same thing. It's micro-wave radio, about ten-centimeter wave. Anything of any size reflects the waves and makes a difference in reception. They use them as a meteor detector on small ships. Big battleships, of course, are protected by those space-disk repulsion effects."

"Hm-m-m! Seems interesting to think that those four-foot steel walls will stop anything man ever sent, and meteors could wander through them practically unhindered."

"Not quite that bad, Spence," Aarn replied. "I'll bet you have been inculcated with that same doctrine that the spaceship designers always had. I never stopped to think about it till I was working on that magnetic atmosphere. Lead is a better protection against meteors than steel. A meteor's kinetic energy is so great it could plow through something like forty-five feet of steel, following the usual law of penetration—varying as the square on the velocity.

"But here's the trick: a meteor plows into the steel, and has to overcome not only the tensile strength of the metal, but the far greater inertia resistance.

Even to ordinary bullets that means something. Remember that water will deflect a bullet like a solid body. Water will flow freely, and so would steel under the impact of a meteor, but it has inertia, and so acts like a solid body, and, as you know, a meteor hole is seldom found to be anywhere near the size of the body that made it.

"What happens is that a one-inch meteor strikes, and the steel resists it with its inertia; each steel crystal acts as a resisting medium and must be accelerated out of the path of the meteor. But the impact generates such heat that the steel molecules are smashed into the vapor state and evaporate. The explosion of expanding iron vapor is what tears a hole.

"I've seen a one-inch meteor leave a three-foot hole through six-inch armor. And then never get inside the ship! It was blown into vapor along with the wall of the ship. So probably that four-foot armor would stop the average meteor and be torn wide open in the process. I'm working on something of the sort—too—"

"Another secret, I suppose?" Spencer put in bitterly.

"Probably," Carlisle agreed blithely. "Come into my lab; I'll show you something interesting. I'm getting on the way now."

It was some five days later that, seated comfortably in the quarters that had been assigned to Spencer, rooms carved from living rock and carefully and artistically decorated with friezes, Carlisle and Spencer were disturbed, nay, even startled, to see a black object the size and general shape of a football come floating gently into the room, turn a cold and unwinking glass eye on them, and say in a slightly cracked voice:

"If you two asteroids with planetary ambitions will arise and follow me down the corridor, I can show you where men of brains are laboring."

Then it fell silent. It stared at them for some seconds as they sat in stupefied amazement, then turned leisurely about and started out of the door. Its cracked voice commented only that:

"Two such frog-mouthed, ant-brained, instinct-controlled, undernourished runts weren't worth the trouble, anyway."

"Well, I'll be a hyperbolic-orbited asteroid. That grease glob from Jupiter has a new idea."

With which Spencer tore out of the door and down the corridor after the fast-vanishing black ostrich egg. Carlisle was on his heels as the soft black of the device all but hid it in the slight gloom of the corridor leading to Aarn's quarters.

Aarn was seated grinning before a television board of a new and complex type.

"Rather clever thing, isn't it?" asked Aarn and the egg at the same time.

"Which of you should I answer?" asked Spencer sarcastically. "That egg up there looks more intelligent. I thought it was a bomb getting ready to blow up when the blamed thing floated in there."

"Yes—we are thinking of that idea, and Anto Rayl, here, has already turned the plans of this device over to his government, and they are making a number of them. Present idea is that after a Shal torpedo has breeched the walls of the ship, these can sail in and start operating on the internal structure as directed.

"This particular model is the new-type spy ship. It consists of miniature—very miniature—spaceship drive of the momentum-wave type, two small but powerful aggie power coils, a radio-control apparatus, and a small radio-sending apparatus connected with a television device of the usual sort—but smaller size. Rather crude. Not a good lining on the screen, but you can see enough, and the ears are quite effective. The whole report is sent back continuously on two short-wave beams.

"As I said, Anto Rayl has turned the plans over to the government, and they are making about ten an hour now. They plan to increase the production to about fifty an hour, and equip all ships with them. The *Sunbeam* is assigned to special duty—with seven full-fledged momentum drive, antigravity-powered battleships and twenty of the new cruisers. Our duty is to patrol and investigate, by any means possible, the doings of Teff-el. The battleships and cruisers are to protect us."

"And you will start hunting for the Data Plates?"

"Absolutely!" replied Munro joyfully. "And find 'em if the Tefflans know where they are—because a number of the professors of languages on Magya, here, have taken the trouble to learn Tefflani—records of their ships and so forth, both written and oral.

"But—you don't yet know the beauties of this television device. This is my real invention, and I'm proud of it. They've said it couldn't be done. You notice the absolute lack of color on the screen—just the greenish white and black of the cathode fluorescence. I can't get any color on this thing ordinarily. There are really two television devices. One for normal operation, and one—"

The television screen went suddenly blank as Aarn pressed a button. A second passed, a faint click from the loudspeaker over the control board, then the screen was lighted again—on a weird scene. It was still the same room they were in, still the screen showed them sitting and standing as before—but now they shone, and the walls of the room glowed in light reflected, light emanating from the men.

"Infra-infra-infra red." Aarn sighed. "Long heat. And what a triumph that is! That's one of the biggest things I ever did. That was a real problem, and I want you to know it. With that, television can operate in absolute darkness!"

"That man passes my understanding," said Carlisle in awe. "His mentality is beyond the comprehension of sane minds. His psychology is not to be analyzed. He builds a space ship that defies gravity; he powers it with energy stolen from the Sun; he defends it with space, warped beyond passing; drives it by meshing in the fabric of space—and goes into raptures over his cleverness in making a fool television eye. It passeth understanding!"

"No; it doesn't, Carlisle. It's all reasonable enough. Physics had known for years that antigravity fields were possible. They knew that power beams were a possibility, that momentum waves were theoretically possible."

"But they said that a heat-eye was theoretically impossible. I can't see how it was done myself."

"Principle of the ordinary television tube. Deposit of metal in globules, discharged by a cathode beam, and effecting a condenser action. Only in this case, my globules are bimetal globules, and one of them acts as might be expected under radiant heat, and throws off electrons. Same idea. An ordinary thermopile in effect, but that each element is about one ten millionth of an inch in diameter, and weighs about one ten billionth of an ounce. The result is rapid reaction. And I have a lens of a special type which will bend those long heat rays. It's really a permanent space structure like that invisibility device. It bends any incident radiation—any radiation—and so can be used equally well on ultraviolet and sub-red."

"It's a strong weapon for finding our data. But—what are you going to do when you find them?" asked Carlisle. "That's not going to help there."

"Grrrr—must you bring up unpleasant subjects when I'm happy?" demanded Munro. "We're going to make a direct raid in secret, then—and do our damnedest to get those plates. That's all we can do."

CHAPTER XII

THE *SANTIR RANLA* AND the *Toal Deenar* had combined in their efforts to crush with the least possible delay, and the least necessary expenditure of energy, the presumptuous heavy cruiser the Tefflans had sent out to investigate the doings of the Magyan fleet that was hanging grimly outside their maximum effective beam-range.

Since the *Santir Ranla* and the *Toal Deenar* were both first-class, new, fully armed battleships, with special alloy-steel armor which had been altered by the addition of a few new elements till the Tefflan standard beam didn't disintegrate it, they crushed the cruiser within forty-five seconds and cut it up for transportation back to the hard-working steel plants on Magya. Every little bit helped.

Aarn went back to work. Anto Rayl and several other Magyans were in the control room of the *Sunbeam* with him as he sent out his little "egg-boat," as the investigators had been called, and attempted to land it on Teff-el safely. He met with difficulties as usual, and cursed the Tefflan ship heartily.

Teff-el was nearly a million miles away, which meant his control of the little machine was extremely poor, since the lightspeed messages that controlled it took several precious seconds for the round trip. He had to move it slowly, exploring carefully before him. Already the little ship was nearer Teff-el than any Magyan had ever been.

The egg-boats, as made in quantity, were egg-shaped, and about eight inches in greatest dimension. They contained no apparatus for the projection of speech, as no attempts would be made to attract attention—decidedly the opposite. Since they were black, Aarn had carefully chosen to send them in from the day side of Teff-el; they were therefore black against black space.

The present egg-boat was within about fifty miles of the surface of the planet when Aarn had been forced, by the lightning swoop of the Tefflan heavy cruiser, to move rapidly to other regions and had moved out of the little investigator's beam. He'd picked it up again, to find the thing was headed for a body of water, and though he'd sent a reversing message, he feared he was too late.

"Blast that restriction on the speed of light! I can't get anywhere this way," he grumbled. "I'll have to send another one now, and every time one of those things is spotted by a Tefflan, it will mean another three hours' work."

"Why not lower a whole collection at once?" suggested Anto Rayl.

"Why—that might be possible—they'd have to respond to two wave lengths—a master wave, that they all obeyed, and a key wave, that they reacted to individually, but it might be done. Canning!" he called suddenly. "Hey—Canning—see if—"

He turned back to the screen as he explained and watched the body of water coming steadily closer. Suddenly it stopped.

"Ah—in time to save Investigator No. 1. Now to see what can be seen. We'll have to explore the planet a bit. You say that Cantak is their largest city, and near here, so I'm going to find a cave or something that I can use to hide that bunch in when we land them."

Rapidly the sea sped behind the lens of the little investigator, and as it finally picked out a dim, distant foreland, Aarn sent a stop signal, followed by a slow.

In minutes a rocky, savage coast was in view, a mass of piled rocks, an ideal location for such a cave as Aarn wanted.

"Are the tides on that world high? I shouldn't think so."

"Very low," replied Anto Rayl. "The single moon is small and distant."

"I don't think water would damage those things any, but I don't intend to try."

The scene on the screen moved slowly along, very little faster than a walk, lest the investigator pass a good spot, or run into a sudden jutting point before Aarn could stop it.

"Canning!" he called suddenly, pushing the stop button of his control. "I'm going to take a chance on their finding that darned thing and stick in an antigravity device, so that it can't run into things and smash itself. I can't creep all over the whole blasted planet like a snail with rheumatism. Fix up those others and bring them out as fast as you can."

"Yes, sir. I've got that radio device fixed up now. It wasn't much trouble—just another coil. I can't quite tell you which one will react to which key wave length, because they are so much alike, but you can pick 'em out. I'll stick to an antigravity coil—if I can find any room."

Aarn turned back to his control, to see the mouth of a great black cavern looming exactly before the eye of his investigator. A great split ran up the cliff, and high above, out of sight, closed in, but it made a narrow cleft cave.

"Ah—luck at last!" he sighed.

He pressed a series of controls and waited.

Presently the screen went blank, shifted, and lighted again with the strange distortion of the heat-eye. The black of the cavern was suddenly light as the investigator entered slowly, and followed it back at a pace of about three feet a second.

Aarn punched a control viciously as a sudden right-angle loomed up ahead. Calmly the investigator drifted on, and on. Then, with a tinkling crash from the loudspeaker mounted with the screen, the view went dead. The hum of the mechanism went on uninterruptedly, as well as the roar of the surf outside the cave; but the screen remained blank, and a slight straining note sounded in the apparatus. The drive was trying to move the cliff.

Aarn pushed a second control with a prayer, and waited. A slight change in the tempo of the sound in the loudspeaker came after a few moments, then a click, a soft hum—and things went on as before.

"Lost! Television-control tube gave way, evidently. They weren't made too well, I'm afraid, too much of a hurry, and with any severe jar, they give way. The rest of the thing's all right. And as useful as a left-hand thread bolt when a right-hand is needed."

"I've got six of those things rigged up, Dr. Munro," announced Canning. "Those small antigravity coils for storing power can be modified a bit, and I used one of the power-storage coils as an antigravitor. You have more than enough power left, haven't you?"

"Certainly, Canning! That's good. Send 'em out. What's the master wave?"

"Eleven point five-five. I'll give you the key-wave list—"

This time, the cave in the cliff was reached easily and safely, a dry floor found well back, and the investigator left. One was brought out on the key wave and immediately started toward Cantak, back in the mountains. It struck a road presently, a broken, rutted track of concrete, with an occasional pedestrian of the Tefflan race. Instinctively, to his surprise, Spencer felt the short hairs on the back of his neck rise, and a wave of anger swept over him at the sight.

"The monsters!" he said in a low tense voice.

Anto Rayl chuckled. "You are a human," he said; "you cannot help that feeling. I know them, have seen them—and hate them more with every sight. Yet I know that they are reasonable, intelligent creatures; that they are no more cruel or evil than we; but our hatred for them is as instinctive and as complete as the hatred of anseth and carlee."

"Cat and dog," said Aarn. "We're born that way; so are they."

The investigator shot rapidly ahead now, in clear daylight, high in the sky. There were ships up here—ships that scurried busily across the sky between cities. There was a great deal of anxious activity, and the furnaces that stood aboveground, alone of Tefflan city structures, were evidently working hard. A great opening in the ground, into which ships of all sizes were constantly sinking while others rose from it, betrayed the entrance to Cantak.

The investigator crept forward at a speed of some two feet per second, till it was directly over the great bore. Then Aarn let it drift across.

By far the most common vessels were huge. The next was. The little investigator caught by it, lodged in a crack under its great, stubby wing, and carried down, cushioned by its antigravity field. Aarn gave a stop signal and knew the little machine would remain in place unless heavily jarred in landing.

The ship it clung to descended, landing in the midst of a great terminal, a bustle of Tefflan activity. With a sudden swoop, the investigator detached itself, shot straight up into the air, and disappeared in the black roof of the great cavern before the startled Tefflans could guess what had happened.

Laborers, common Tefflans, they paid no further attention, and went on with their work. And all that day, behind doors, hidden in great vessels, in small vases and among bushes in parks, the investigator listened and watched and sought. It crept out when the lights were turned down for the rest period, and slunk into important public buildings, buildings that had no window glass in this great cavern where there was no weather, save that which they made themselves. Through ventilation tubes, through doors, through transoms, the investigator went, seeking records, secrets—

Never before had Magyans had so perfect an opportunity to learn every secret of Teff-el. But they could not read the records they so much wanted. They listened to a chance conversation between officers on the merchant stratosphere ships, and spaceship warrior officers. And learned only that no Tefflan save those few who manufactured the essential parts knew of the secret of the ray, and the reason it was made so great a secret was that no known apparatus would stop the effect of the ray.

—◇—

It was night now, and the public buildings were all but entirely closed; a lone watchman wandering about here and there was the only sign of life as the investigator went silently through the various corridors, occasionally bumping noiselessly against a dead end until turned by a new radio signal—a curious thing that seemed blind to its surroundings, blundering here and there, and learning this and that.

"I think that new plan to attack the Magyans will be wholly successful—a thing they cannot resist. Ah, if we but had brought Magya that strange new destructive ray! Without it, we would have—need—" The voice trailed off into a maze of roaring traffic sounds.

"The new ships, you understand, will have a hollow center, and the center-explosion bombs of the Magyans will be useless. The magnetic bombs we will deflect easily now, with the new apparatus of Hoo Ralsop, and tune them instead—"

"Some have suggested that those strangers who came in the ship attacked by the scouting squadron, when first the destructive, fusing beam was used, were some of the surviving, ancient Ma-jhay-anhy of legend, who came through. Perhaps they were messengers—but they had such war craft that surely the Teff-Hellani—our own race on its native world—must have grown equally great in power.

"Hoo Ralsop is working now, they say, to devise a means of at least signalling through—"

"I'd like," commented Aarn in annoyance, "to know who in the name of the nine wabbling worlds that Hoo Ralsop is and, more important, where he is. He seems to be a prominent scientist, and if he's working on communication between spaces, his aims and mine are parallel, and I'll bet a major planet to an asteroid, he's got at least an accurate copy of those Data Plates.

"Could he read 'em, Anto Rayl?"

"Probably, in time. We could read them with a little study, and with the aid of your knowledge of the other side. Hoo Ralsop would be laboring under the difficulties of not having our knowledge of ancient Magyan language, and complete ignorance of the other side. He will, of course, have the assistance of a knowledge of modern Magyan, but the language has altered beyond understanding, almost, and it was only after great study, and careful consideration of the ways in which languages do change, and the following back of our more modern tongues, that we were able to read the ancient records. Hoo Ralsop would have a heavy, but possible, task."

"Might they not have translated it already?"

"Why should they? They had no great interest in it before they found us in modern times; it was merely loot of ancient days which they had been told was sacred, and to be kept. After they found us—I think I am not too boasting in saying we occupied their attention rather fully. Their linguists were busy trying to keep pace with the various codes we adopted in giving our sealed orders to ship commanders. We have some ancient Tefflan records—in Teff-Hellani really—that we have never translated, beyond finding what they mean. But is that important?"

"Decidedly! I don't want a few battleships of the kind Tefflans are used to going over and attacking our commerce in the other world. Good Heaven, they could wipe out half the population there—we have no real defensive machines. Of course we could build them in a few years, but Tefflan battleships attacking wouldn't give us a few years.

"If Hoo Ralsop can act on that data very quickly, we're going to find out who and where Hoo Ralsop is—and—we might do that anyway, just for safety. I have a dozen or so of those things made up with equipment to explode them at will, or when tampered with. I think we'd better find out where he is."

"Have you heard the latest news from the government laboratories?" asked a growling Tefflan voice, while a trained translator spoke softly into a microphone the corresponding Magyan words. "Hoo Ralsop has found among some ancient religious relics some plates in what he is sure are ancient Ma-jhay-anhy characters that deal with the crossing from one space to another. The relic plates—"

And on Tefflan, the drifting, seeking investigator had drifted slowly past the office whence had come those voices. Aarn was grimly, silently busy sending it back. Seconds passed. Long, long seconds while nothing happened, and only the strangely lighted scene as shown by radiant heat swept over the screen, and the dull sound of traffic outside, activated the instruments. The thing stopped, swung, and started back. Instantly Aarn pushed the stop signal. It would take equally long for that signal to get there—

"—naturally wouldn't let him take them out. They were sacred relics, and protected apparently by an ancient legend that some day they would lead our race to greatness and a land of plenty once more. This prophecy had protected them through hundreds of thousands of moons, and they had been made of a metal which would endure, so they were quite legible.

"Hoo Ralsop has called in Sol Kaldan to aid him in his research, and surely with such a student of physics and such a student of languages, we shall learn something of import, for the plates evidently have been considered of importance from oldest times. Hoo Ralsop's copies are exact as can be, even to microscopic dents and scratches."

"But what does he hope to learn, what does he think might come of such a search in legends ages old? Truly, once we could learn from the ancients, but now our weapons pass theirs manyfold," replied the second voice.

Aarn dared not try to look at the speakers behind the half-opened door.

"That, he believes, is the secret of the ones who came in the strange ship, bringing the strange weapon. Remember, the controller of the destroyer which escaped their blasting ray said he saw them materialize suddenly as though sweeping in from infinite distance with infinite velocity—yet there was something lacking in that conception, since they seemed rather to expand from infinite smallness, and not move at all. He was certain, though, that they came in no normal way."

"The physicist of Santakalt says they came from this other space."

"Then why—but stay—look you—that magnetometer is fluctuating with my speech, and with other signals, too. What can that mean? Ehu—it shows a center of force near here! I don't like it. Let us see—ha—it is near, too—"

Frantically, and yet resignedly, Aarn had pressed the signal that would send the little investigator away at its best speed, within such narrow confines. He sent a complete series of signals which would have freed it from the building, by driving out of an open window, but the Tefflan suddenly appeared in the door.

"Hayuu—look! What manner of thing is that?" He reached for it, and the little investigator sheered away. "Ha—it has some manner of control. Now what can be the meaning of this?"

He darted back into his room and reappeared a moment later with a device the size and shape of two pie plates stuck together, and trailing a long cord.

"Let us see—"

The investigator suddenly darted for the pieplate device, in fact a powerful electromagnet, and stuck. Aarn sighed and pressed a red button on one side.

Some fifteen seconds later the Tefflans were wrestling with the struggling, pulling little investigator, as it sought to obey the commands. Then, suddenly, the screen went dark in a sudden flash of light. The little investigator on Teff-el turned bright red, and sputtered sharply with blue electric flame.

"That is the end of that!" said Aarn, but he wasn't much disappointed, for he had learned at least that the records still existed. "Now—problem one is to find this Hoo Ralsop. They mentioned 'the physicist of Santakalt,' and I just wondered if that might be he."

"It is." Anto Rayl nodded. "I remember that some of the reports we have found on destroyed ships have stated that that city was their scientific base, and a division of Santakaruck, their main spaceship base."

"Next—where is Santakaruck?"

"That, too, is known, of course, and we can send the next investigator there—but how will you find Hoo Ralsop?"

Aarn smiled suddenly, a smile that wandered clear across his face. "That," he said, "will be easy if he's as important as all that. Watch!"

He started an investigator out of the base in the cave, flew it swiftly toward Santakaruck and, when it was on its way, switched to the key wave of a second investigator and started it close in the wake of the first. Aarn was very busy for the next few minutes, in fact till he had both motionless just outside of Santakaruck.

Then he started a curious process. The investigators had been equipped with small gas-glow lights in case they had to see something where no light and insufficient heat was available. And now Aarn waited till a scout ship started in the great tunnel that led down into Santakaruck, then turned on the light on one of the investigators, and started the ship cruising in circles slowly down into the great opening of Santakaruck.

While the first was slowly and aimlessly proceeding automatically on this order, he shifted to the second device. In seconds he was watching the scout ship stop and then begin a series of movements to investigate the strange, tiny ship. They had it presently and bound it down tightly.

In triumph they bore their prize into the city, and attached closely to a part of their landing gear where it was nearly invisible was the second investigator.

Like a leech it clung to the trail as the first machine was taken to the spaceship port, investigated by higher, and yet higher, officers with curiosity—while at another receiving board Magyans listened carefully to all that was said there—and at last scientists were called in.

"I think it is a bomb—a sort of self-controlled torpedo," announced a physicist at length.

"Nonsense! The Magyans' brains are not so poor. They built this, surely, and it must be investigated carefully, but no bomb of this size is dangerous. I am interested to know the method of control. They are not being rained on the planet, why, then, did it happen to be here? Were there more?"

"None were seen, most excellent sir."

"Meaning, fool, that you didn't look."

"I stand in the guilt of negligence, most excellent sir," acknowledged the scout-ship commander.

"Ehuu—use your head—and your eyes too, next time. Now—go out and look about."

The scout-ship man left hurriedly.

"I think it is a bomb," persisted the physicist, "and not necessarily a chemical one. Might it not be the store-house of much physical energy—an accumulator? Or a new and unknown kind of power-storage device, a bomb that will go off at any time?"

"More likely," suggested a chemist, "might it not be one of the bombs like those we are preparing—biologic bombs, full of germs; it could do untold damage."

"Ehuu—what unpleasant ideas you have!" exclaimed the most excellent sir, hurriedly releasing the little things, and backing off, wiping his long-fingered hands. "Can you test it?"

"I think it would be better," suggested the chemist, "to call our masters. This is indeed important. I believe that Hoo Ralsop would be interested, for this may be an idea of those from the other side."

"That's interesting," said Spencer, "what they had to say about biologic bombs. Could they make them?"

"Oh, decidedly! They must have done it already."

"That is all well, Aarn," said Anto Rayl contentedly. "We are preparing already. How great will be their joy when they learn that their discussion has reached us in its entirety!"

"Sorry, Anto Rayl, but they won't. If I let Hoo Ralsop get so much as a glimpse of the interior, he'll know a number of things it isn't good for little Tefflans to know—such as how to make an antigravity power coil," Aarn pointed out.

"Hoo Ralsop says he will come, but is much annoyed, since we disturbed him in a perusal of the ancient plates," said an assistant as he returned from a telephonic device.

He stooped momentarily, to pull something from between the halves of his left hoof, and suddenly started.

"By holy Renoo! That is no blank hole in the end—there is some potent force at work which twists light—distorts it. By all my physics, I swear it! That is a lens!"

"What? A lens? It is merely a magnetic-force wall of some kind!" scoffed a second Tefflan. "Light does not bend so readily as that—it requires some substance."

"Silence—listen to me!" snapped the discoverer of the force-lens. "I say that it is a lens. We shall see what Hoo Ralsop says, and, till then, say no more. If it is a lens—then this is a bomb. It is a bomb which will blow us up with our own words—it is a spy machine—a device to slip about and learn, from our own lips and laboratories, our secrets. Probably something went wrong with the mechanism that made it go off its course and be discovered. If that be so, then surely it has ears as well as eyes. It may be sending back a beam of radio information at this instant. Put something over that eye."

In an instant a container of some sort shut out the light from the investigator. But though silence fell, a few moments later the second investigator, outside the room, showed a group of three Tefflans trotting toward the office. Their hoofs made almost no noise on the soft, rubberlike flooring, but evidently the men inside the room knew they were approaching, for they opened the door. The light streamed out into the less brilliantly lighted corridor, and would have illuminated the second investigator had it not been clinging to the ceiling, above eye level, and above the light.

Hoo Ralsop was aware of his importance. And he was justly, perhaps, annoyed. "For what cause, Aggar Mankel, have you summoned me from my investigation of the Kakkakill relic plates?" And he said part of a further sentence, which, due to the peculiarity of Tefflan word-order, would translate something like this:

"Other-space secrets from Kakkakill relic plates beginning to learn of greatest—"

"Stop! Do not speak—this device is some machine whereby the unnatural ones, the Magyans, can listen and watch us."

The cloud of anger that had swept crimson over Hoo Ralsop's normally red face disappeared as suddenly as it had come. "Ehuu—what is this? Let me see this!"

———————◆———————

Some two seconds ago Aarn had pressed the button that converted the little investigator into a red-hot mass of metal that would glow for several hours. Hoo Ralsop was looking into the force-lens with great interest when it collapsed with a report of inrushing gases, and the metal in his hands flowed red-hot abruptly. With a curse of pain he dropped it to the floor.

"By the nine greatest gods, the thing has burned me! May the soul of its designer rot forever in the lowest level of the filthiest hell! The damnable thing—may it be accursed forever—has taken half the flesh from my hands!" Hoo Ralsop glared at it with slit eyes blazing in anger, his raw hands agonizing.

"Most gracious and learned sir, let me dress the wounds," begged a humble doctor, who was presently gathering a small kit from the lockers just outside the doorway.

"Dress them, you clumsy fool, and if you do a poor job, I shall have you condemned to the prison of Carcatoon for incompetency. As it is, my work will be held up—"

Aarn had not been idle during this time. He had been busy, indeed, with a second control board. And he was prepared now to interrupt Hoo Ralsop's speech.

An investigator two feet long and a foot in diameter entered through the doorway, and stopped in the center of the room. Hoo Ralsop's speech broke off in amazement, he stood paralyzed for seconds, and the ship finished it for him: "Forever!" it said in a cracked, metallic voice and perfect Tefflani. There was a dull click, the machine grew slowly red, brighter red—

"It will explode," gasped the scientist and dived for the door. The machine was white-hot now—and the scene vanished in a roar of flame.

"That," said Aarn contentedly, "destroyed the cavern for half a mile around, I suspect, for the coils in that little thing had plenty of power."

The screen lighted up again presently—again in the cave by the seaside. It was light there now, distant Anrel shining in, bright blue.

"Kakkakill seems to be our next destination," said Spencer. "Where is it, Anto Rayl?"

"I might have guessed where we'd find those plates. I should have thought more seriously of finding it by thought. The city of Kakkakill is their holy city. Kak-ka is their principal god. He is their god of victory.

"And he is their one genuine bad point to which we can point with reasonable loathing. There is a ceremonial of consecration to him each thirteen moons—each time their moon makes thirteen circuits. It is called the 'Death of Time' or 'Death of Time Unit' festival. And in that consecration they must drink to Kak-ka in the blood of a captured foe, and eat of the flesh of a captured foe, or they eat of the flesh and drink of the blood of one of their own race—a young female usually is sacrificed if need be.

"But if they capture a foe, and lose the engagement in which the foe is captured, then they cannot sacrifice that foe to Kak-ka, for he is the god of victory."

"They lost their last battle with us. One of their own females will be sacrificed this time—the sacrifice is due in one and a half moons."

Aarn was interested—decidedly. "That is not so good. It is interesting—thirteen moons is the length of the year in the other space. The year is the time unit there, and this sacrificial festival must have been brought over with them; the 'Death of the Year' was what it was called back there, I suspect. The consecration was probably intended to bring them victory during the next year—a logical time division on Earth, since the year has important climatic manifestations there.

"But if those plates are there—we'll have to raid—and they'd be extraordinarily glad to see us—"

"I'm afraid," said Anto Rayl soberly, "the plates are there. They have the sacred Temple to Kak-ka, remember, and all the relics. When that ancient

Teff-hellani looted our ancestors of that series of plates, he no doubt turned them over to Kak-ka for protection, to the god who had given him his victory.

"The Temple of Kak-ka is also their greatest museum, for it contains relics that have been given to Kak-ka through all the ages since he was first worshiped on that planet. Now it is, of course, a semi-scientific museum.

"We have no choice, so far as I can see. I'll investigate, of course—I'll have to learn the way, anyhow."

In minutes the investigator had been brought near the entrance to Kakkakill, but bringing it in was a problem, for there were few ships entering and leaving there, and it was daylight now. Most of these ships were small, private machines carrying supplicants to the temple, for Kak-ka was also god of business victory.

Aarn at last hid the investigator and turned in for rest. It was dark in Kakkakill when he had risen and breakfasted. When once more the investigator set out, it penetrated through the tunnels easily now.

When the investigator, entering from a great, tall, cathedral-like tunnel, with great stone arches, carved and lighted with glowing blue and green, strangely beautiful effects produced by fluorescent paint and ultraviolet light, came into that main cathedral of Kak-ka, Aarn had to admit himself impressed.

It was a single gigantic cavern, the floor square, four enormous arches soaring up to meet in the center of the roof, nearly one thousand feet above. A dim, dusky glow of violet light seemed to pervade this higher region from thousands of tiny, hidden lights. The walls of the cavern were carved in bas-relief, and the carvings then colored with the skill of a great painter. Each scene represented some great victory in the history of Teff-el, or some great, prehistoric victory of legend.

And in each Kak-ka appeared in the background.

But in the cavern, Kak-ka was in the foreground. It was a statue. A thing breath-taking, awe-inspiring, horrible—and magnificently beautiful. Kak-ka towered a full three hundred feet. He was a Tefflan, of course, but the Tefflan of a Tefflan's ideals. His gigantic face was stern, and powerful—yet inspiring, even to a human. It was turned up, looking onward. One hand was raised on high, with a great sword in it. The other beckoned.

And the whole, gigantic thing was a blazing, faceted ruby. Synthetic, necessarily, but the magnificent, high color, the glow and the fire of the gem was there, and, under the wonderfully skillful lighting, magnificent. Kak-ka's trappings were simple, and all of red-gold and blue-white chromium alloy; his mighty sword glistened like a fiery beacon, and from its tip sprang a beam of golden light that cut a swath through the violet dusk of the upper reaches of that titanic cathedral, a beam of gold, laid on a background of purple velvet.

Between the feet of the colossus was the altar, a single gigantic block of sapphire. Some hidden lights within it made it glow continuously with that inimitable, indescribable blue of the most perfect jewel. And on each side of it burned a steady, unwavering flame of pure white light, frozen radiance, a perfect spindle that stood three feet high.

Beyond and behind the image of Kak-ka was the temple. It had been carved of some white stone, a marble, perhaps, which stood out like a white crystal box in this cavern in dark rock.

"I never dreamed," said Anto Rayl softly, "that those Tefflans were capable of such magnificent things. We have our Temple City—but it cannot compare with that. I can almost forgive them their monstrous forms while I look at that scene."

"I—I'll have to look in the museum," said Aarn at length. "And—that will have to be destroyed with the rest of Teff-el. I think if it alone was saved, posterity would blame you for destroying the race that could create it."

CHAPTER XIII

"OUR SHIPS," AARN WAS explaining, "must be small enough to be almost invisible, yet large enough to have the power we need. And for that fool chemical apparatus Carlisle put in. You said I should get an explanation of that soon—"

"Uh-huh! Just paying you back some of your own. You can wait till we're ready this time." Spencer nodded with a grin.

"Well—the ships are made. And, after that glimpse we got of Kakkakill, I've done something—I've had them painted with a smoky violet color that will make them almost invisible in the higher reaches of that place. It's so darned dim in there they won't spot us, and we can make use of televisors for sight, and have no lights visible."

"Are those televisors going to be equipped with heat-eye apparatus?"

"Certainly, and we'll need them. Remember how dark it was in that particular vault. They are demountable. We can take them out of their port hole in a few seconds, and use them to guide us around without the necessity of lights. They weigh only about as much as one of those pistols—and look out how you aim those pistols, by the way, they'll blow up anything within fifty feet of you so hard they'll probably hurt you—and they will enable us to get along without light."

"Uhmm—wonder if they're any good?" said Spencer, picking up one of the compact oblong devices Aarn had gestured toward.

He picked it up, pushed a stud, and watched an image form on the view-plate with perfect clarity, but with the typical appearance of a heat-image. Spencer pulled something the size of a hen's egg from his pocket, held it out at arm's length, and dropped it gracefully.

It hit with a dull, hollow plop, and burst into an instant, spreading blackness! In a fraction of a second the room was in utter blackness, a jet night so intense that the powerful glow lamps of the laboratory were utterly lost. There was nothing but a solid, impenetrable wall of blankness.

"Good lord, what is that?" gasped Aarn. "Hey—where in blazes are you? I can't—say, I can't see my hand when it's touching my face. Uh—here's a light now—"

Silence. A chuckle from Spencer. "It won't work—"

"Haw!" Spencer looked at the screen of his heat-eye televisor, and grinned wider.

As though through a slight, bright fog, he could see Aarn, shining brightly, and holding a flash-lamp that was shining equally brightly, but seemed to be curiously affected by the fog. "It's working. It just can't light, can't send a beam. Put it about half an inch from your eye, and you can see it."

Aarn did. "Sweet singing satellites—what a fog that ink makes! What in space is it?"

"Infra-infra-infra fluorescence." Spencer grinned. "And your heat-eye works beautifully. That's what friend Carlisle made for the occasion of our raid. The chemical tanks contain a load of this. It combines with the oxygen of the air to form a chemical dye in particles so tiny they are close to the brownian limits, and won't settle out in less than about three hours under Teff-el's gravity."

"Infra-infra—and so forth. I think I commence to understand. Will you kindly supply me with one of those heat-visors so I can see my way out? What do you do to use it in this?"

"Stick it so close to your eyes, and turn it up so far that you can see it. This fog isn't utterly impenetrable, you know."

"No—but if I am right, it would be darned near it. I take it that this stuff acts the way fluorescence does with ultraviolet. It takes ultraviolet, and reduces it to visible light. This takes visible, and reduces it to infra-visible. Right?"

"Quite right. The heat-visor is somewhat obscured, because that re-radiation of heat by the little particles of the dye makes a foglike breaking up of the light, and also the heat."

"Hmmm—but this will be handy, indeed. Now I'll show you the ships."

Aarn led the way, equipped now with a vision device, up to the level where his ships had been stored. They were two specially built spy ships, one-man craft, about ten feet long by three feet in diameter. They were equipped with surprisingly powerful weapons, and were able to exceed the speed of light. Their bulk was practically all taken up by power coils. At the nose was the control compartment, and here the vision devices had been installed.

The controls were standard, save for the release working the darkness device which Carlisle had installed himself. With Spencer's aid, he had arranged it so that streams of the liquid chemical would shoot in all directions from the little ship with tremendous force, making an effective darkness nearly five hundred feet in diameter.

"I don't see why," said Carlisle coming up, "I'm not included in this little venture."

"Excellent reason. Speakum Ainglitch. We might get caught you know—be a good thing if you could skip around—via investigator—and learn what's what with us, and let us tell you so they wouldn't know what our plans were. They know Magyan. They don't know English. Ergo: English is the thing to use."

"And since the Moon is constituted of green cheese— Of course Spence couldn't speak English. You, I'll admit, have advantages, with that mind-under-matter body of yours, that gorilla-patterned, Neanderthal nit-wit construction. But Spence—"

"Spence is a virtuoso of the control board, a master of movements, a commander of the keys. He can turn three back-somersaults, six corkscrew twists, and in inverted double-barreled upside down backward flight while you unravel your eyes from watching him," grinned Aarn. "Sorry, Carlisle—we've got to leave one representative, and I guess you're elected."

"I know it," admitted Carlisle. "Good luck. I'll be watching—"

———⋄———

The two little ships rose, and spun gracefully out through the entrance way, and finally, passing through the lock, into free space. They swooped rapidly away from the great metal side of the battleship, and darted, faster than light, toward Teff-el. Both knew perfectly well that, were they captured, rescue would be beyond any possibility. They were going in two parties, because it doubled their chances of escape, if detected. Spencer would go first, once they landed, for, were he caught, Aarn would make a far more deadly rescue force than Spence.

Faster than light they whirled by the defensive orbital forts, and the savagely circling swift cruisers Teff-el had sent out to watch the Magyan fleet, and whisked into the atmosphere of the planet itself, before the ships were stopped to a planetary speed in mere miles. In that peculiar condition by which speeds greater than that of light were possible, they seemed to be moving at a quite normal rate, they were able to control their motion readily.

In the atmosphere, they slanted down instantly, till their smoke-colored ships were lost against the dark background of night Teff-el. The ships were being driven only by momentum drive now; no antigravity power was used, lest they be detected.

Kakkakill was near. In seconds they dived into the black hold that was the entrance. A sentry ship hung there, watching the incoming traffic, but as the two smoke-colored ships dropped down, they flashed the correct pass signal of light and dropped on unhindered.

Lightless, high in the great dusky dome of the cathedral city they swept on, so close to the ceiling they were bathed in the violet glow of the tiny hidden lamps. From their present position, a dozen other structures were visible, and swiftly the ships dived, when they reached a dimly lighted corner of the great cavern, and with an infinite skill landed noiselessly and lightly on a stone porch of a deserted, lightless prayer house. Not till the great sacrifice time would it be needed. Here the victim would be prepared—

"Let's hope we come back only once," whispered Aarn as he and Spence met outside their ships. "You go ahead."

With the assurance of an inhabitant Spencer swung off along the pathway, his rubber-soled shoes making no sound. The light was dim, a golden mist of light produced by innumerable tiny bulbs hidden from the eye, but casting their soft glow on various objects that gave a gentle diffused glow everywhere. Swiftly, and with assurance, Spence made for the great temple of Kakkakill.

Past the left hoof of the giant ruby statue—it was bound in a shoe of the curious red gold—on toward the Temple, the white marble faintly golden in the light.

No Tefflan moved about here now, for this was the hour when everyone save the watchman slept.

Only far across the great cavern could he see a Tefflan guard at the mouth of each individual cavern. But at that distance Spence looked like a Tefflan himself—for he had on a remarkably clever outfit that seemed to twist his legs and his body.

Behind him somewhere in the eternal golden dusk, Aarn slung along. No art could make his great thickset body seem a Tefflan's so the trick had not been tried. Which was another reason why Spencer went first.

Up the broad stairway, gleaming with more of those hidden projectors of gold and violet light, Spencer went—somewhat worried, for he must show clearly now—and his walk was not the lope of the Tefflan's goatlike legs.

In a moment more he was within the shelter of the great, majestic columns, mighty, square columns that stretched in golden light up into the dusk-violet gloom under the heavy overhanging roof. Like a miniature of the vaster cathedral of the cavern, this overhanging marble ceiling was lined with tiny projectors, and the smoky violet haze hung motionless.

Quickly Spencer slipped on to the next row of pillars and slipped in among them. There were no shadows here—no spots of darkness.

Enormous doors of that reddish gold—the ash of the atomic engines of Teff-el and Magya, he learned later—were swung between great, wondrously carved posts of amethyst, deep, deep violet, illuminated from within. The great golden doors were covered with bas-relief of scenes of mythological import, scenes from the tales of Earth, in the other space, even.

Beyond, inside, Spencer entered the comforting gloom of the deserted Temple. On, past the small prayer chambers, on to the museum beyond. Through a passage that branched in the utter darkness, his steps guided by the heat rays thrown off by his own body, he finally entered the museum section, up a winding ramp, up to the third floor. Right, down a broad corridor, to a room lined with cases and tables.

In the center of the room, ranged under a glass case, were the eleven plates of data, worked out some thirty thousand years before, by a scientist, marooned by inexpressible time and an unimaginable distance from his home world, wondering what its fate might have been.

Something hummed softly in his hand, a slight screeching sounded, then a soft hiss of escaping air. Again the humming, the slight, almost inaudible screech and a third and fourth time. Spencer lifted away in his hands a section of the hard, tough glass, cut out in a rough oblong by the efficient little Magyan cutter he had brought.

Each plate was about a quarter of an inch thick, and about ten inches square. One by one he lifted them out, and began to frown in troubled surprise as he did so. For each plate was heavy! The density of the metal was nearly twenty; each one weighed more than fifteen pounds—considerably more. With a sinking feeling of horror, he realized that this one unconsidered and perfectly simple, physical fact was going to get the expedition into serious trouble. His load was to have been the plates—his duty. But they were mere pages of data—their weight had not been considered. Aarn, far faster, far stronger, was to have been the defensive force. And with that single slip, their plans were thrown off badly. He could not carry something near two hundred pounds of metal plates in his arms. The little sacks he had brought would never bear up under that load.

He stood in momentary surprise and lightning thought. Aarn, with his enormous strength, could easily carry them, of course, but Aarn was to have met him below. There was no watchman in the museum, and he was supposed to get back to the portico where Aarn waited behind a pillar of safety—but if they were forced to make four trips through the museum—

A light tap-tap-tap-tap on the soft, muffling, rubbery composition flooring suddenly attracted him. A sound almost inaudible, so faint he never would have heard it had he not been standing motionless, concentrated on thought and danger. Tefflan hoofs trotting rapidly along—a squad of a dozen of them at least!

With a sudden breath of horrified amazement at his own stupidity, he remembered the hiss of air as he opened the case. The gas in that case had been under pressure as a thief-trap!

"Sweet satellites—what an asteroid brain I've got," he groaned.

He rapidly pulled four darkness bombs from his pocket, threw them to the four corners of the room, and heard them burst with soft plops as the tapping hoofs of the Tefflans approached rapidly. Light appeared down the corridor—then was blotted out by a sudden rising cloud of blackness. Spence picked up his heat-visor, swung up a load of the metal plates in each of his sacks, hoping he had important ones, and slid for the doorway toward the rear—to see a group of Tefflans sliding around the corner into view.

The first group was halted now, stretching hands out into the gloom, seeking to feel something. Sharp, high-pitched voices barked commands back and forth across the room, as the parties acquainted each other of the situation. Both parties were halted now.

They were spread across the doorway, holding hands. One of them was saying something. Probably meant for Spencer—thought him a mere thief no doubt.

Spence looked doubtfully at the man on the end of one row, watched carefully and hopefully, and saw him release the hand of the next man for a second. The hands on the Tefflans were just like his own—same five-fingered hand—not hairy. Spencer smiled grimly and threw two more darkness bombs. Quickly and noiselessly, he sped back and forth carrying his plates, depositing them near the doorway, and making another trip.

Then—he watched. The end man released his neighbor's hand again for an instant, and in that instant Spencer grasped the Tefflan hand with a feeling of surging anger and loathing. With the other, his right, he snapped down hard on the back of the strange, thin neck, thanking Aarn's forethought in arranging a headpiece that would hold his heat-visor in place without use of hands.

Just the edge of his palm—the Tefflan's neck was soft—and skillfully wielded as it was, with a knowledge of Tefflan skeletons, it was instantaneously, soundlessly fatal. The spinal cord severed before the creature was aware of danger, he slumped, lowered by Spencer's grasping fingers, which were wound in the loathsome, coarse hair that seemed to have individual, noisome life.

Then he realized suddenly that the Tefflan on his side was saying something—asking something. Spencer knew he could never risk language—he was half stooping, that position had attracted the other's attention, but now, Spencer was busy arranging the plates on the other side of the doorway.

———◇———

With a sudden startled shriek, as of terrified surprise, Spencer dived into the museum room, pulled the Tefflan with him—then releasing his hold and instantly stepping back. With a single, terrific heave he sent the body of the dead Tefflan flying into the room on the heels of the now-staggering line of excited, shouting, Tefflan guards.

"So long; you're the goats for sure, this time!"

Spencer was on his way. The plates were a staggering load—but he had them all. The Tefflans were creating a terrific fuss at finding the dead body of their companion inside the room. The line had been re-formed instantly, but now they were sure that someone was inside that room, and had killed one of their number.

Spencer was rapidly retracing his steps. He reached the main corridor that led from the museum proper to the prayer rooms without trouble, save for his staggering load. His arms were aching, his breath labored, and he knew he must stop soon. If only he could have packed those plates properly—

And he passed, unseeing, a guard who stood half concealed in the doorway of a side passage. Instantly the Tefflan was out. But he paused in stupefied paralysis for a second before he struck. The thief was not a Tefflan! He was a Magyan!

A mighty roar of warning—a cry of the information, and the Tefflan was on Spencer. Before he could drop his burden, powerful arms were wrapped about him. He fell, with the weight of the plates added. In ten seconds of struggling he freed himself of the plates, and in another five seconds, the Tefflan guard was flying through the air to smash with a broken neck.

Like jujitsu in the Occident, Apache kicking in the orient, boxing was unknown here. The Tefflan, however, had done his work. The squad above had heard, and had heard that a Magyan was among them! A Magyan, and the Death of the Year sacrifice so near—

A score of Tefflans came galloping down the ramps, and Spencer threw the last of his darkness bombs. Instantly he realized that his heat-vision apparatus had been so thoroughly ruined he had been looking through an empty framework! He was as blind as the Tefflans.

With a groan he picked up his load of plates and set off as best he could. "Aarn will be coming—I'd better let him take these plates and beat it for the ship—"

Somewhere ahead a tremendous clang of metal sounded. With a start of surprise Spencer realized the huge grille of golden bars that hung before the main entrance had been lowered to bar his escape—and Aarn's entrance!

Half a dozen groping arms reached him simultaneously, as he reached the end of the black hall. Instantly the plates were dropped, and the nearest Tefflan howled in agony as the heavy metal broke a bone.

"Look out, weakling," said a deep voice, just beside Spencer.

A Tefflan rose suddenly from the ground, darted forward with speed so great he was a blur, and smashed against two of his comrades—horribly.

"The plates—all there—weigh two hundred pounds—no heat-visor—no light bombs—"

Spencer uppercut a Tefflan, and suddenly realized that though they didn't have boxing, they had their own peculiar system. It depended on the fact that they had horns—and it was very deadly. With wonderful adroitness Aarn raised his heavily booted, thick-muscled leg and planted his foot on a Tefflan skull. The Tefflans stopped attempting to use their horns after that demonstration.

The Jovian moved like a bouncing ball of deadly destruction. His muscles found this planet's gravity weak, his thirty-foot bounds carried him in and out of the fight while his slower, weaker opponents saw him only as a flash of deadly striking flesh.

Aarn didn't use his hands alone. He used his legs, too. He didn't use his fists because long since he had learned his muscles were too strong for the bones. He used his forearm with a chopping motion, and realized rather wonderingly that the Tefflans' necks weren't as tough as a Terrestrian's.

In some thirty-five seconds the fight was over—the remaining Tefflans being strewn all up the hall as Aarn charged after them. They could run more swiftly on their goat feet than any Terrestrian, but the Jovian charged after them in great bounds.

Spencer was sitting down, very busy being sick. "They—they're awful," he gasped when Aarn returned. "Let's get away."

"Uh-huh! Good idea," said Aarn. "Better do it fast. Those fellows were sort of police. Guess you set off some kind of alarm. They thought it was a thief and didn't carry weapons." He picked up all the plates, some two hundred pounds of them, under his left arm, tucked his heat-visor under the other, and started off at a lope toward the doorway.

"We can't get out, I heard that grate fall."

"So did I. That's the only way I know to get out, though, so out we go," replied Aarn. They reached it in seconds, and the Jovian set down the plates tenderly and looked at the grate. The metal bars were an inch and a half thick.

"Uhhh—bad. That's gold. Residue from their atomic engines. Sort of an ash. It's as good a conductor as copper, but heavy, and a bit soft. The point is it's a good conductor." Aarn had lifted his heavy weapon, and pointed it at the junction of two of the crossed metal bars. "We'll see—"

The ball of blue electric force traveled straight and true, hit the junction, and was followed by about fifty others. The metal bars glowed red-hot—for several feet around.

"No go. The stuff won't melt, because it conducts both current and heat too well. I can't use any more powerful magnetic balls on it, because the stuff won't absorb them. So that leaves—"

Aarn walked rapidly to the opposite side of the great grille, and examined it carefully. The bars were in two planes, and those running vertically were a little nearer than those running horizontally. Deliberately Aarn took hold of two of the bars, and settled his squat, thick body comfortably.

"Keep your ears open," he said briefly—and went to work. The fine, elastic cloth of his shirt suddenly bulged into tortured ridges that ran across his shoulders, and up his neck, and down to his hips. Huge wide strands of muscles rose and writhed and strained, muscles such as Hercules might have had, or Samson. Trained by a life time on the giant of the solar system, they were the muscles of a giant. They strained, and slowly, inevitably, the heavy metal bars bent and turned, and suddenly sprang from their sockets.

Slowly Aarn straightened and stretched himself. He pulled the bars out of the way. "About two more—" He grasped a horizontal bar now, and began straining upward. His legs now took the strain. The muscles like broad, smooth, rubber springs lifted themselves into ridges—and the great metal bar snapped out of its socket.

"Reënforcements, I take it," said Aarn, as he crawled through the gap.

He threw down a dozen of the anti-light bombs, and in the darkness took the metal plates as Spencer passed them through. Somewhere a steady marching tread was coming, the tread of several hundred feet. "We can't argue with the royal army."

Spencer dived through the gap in the grille, and suddenly realized that one of their own investigator machines was hovering near them. Aarn saw it, and with a sudden leap grabbed it, and handed it to Spencer. "Carlisle can guide you to your ship with that—just follow its movements, and I won't have to lead you."

He had his heat-visor on and started off. For a few seconds the little investigator did not move, then Spencer felt it pulling steadily in the same direction Aarn was going and followed rapidly. Aarn was dropping bombs rapidly, and despite the best efforts of the soldiery, he was avoiding them skillfully. Spencer was in worse plight, for Carlisle, millions of miles away, could not see and avoid the soldiers in time, and while the investigator would lead him to the ship, he had to look out for himself.

One soldier blundered against him—and died with a croak. Before a comrade found him Spencer got away.

⸻ ◆ ⸻

After long minutes, they reached their ships, Aarn was already in, and had deposited the plates when Spencer got there.

"Here's an extra heat-visor," said Aarn, handing the device to the engineer. "Snap it in. Turn loose your blackness."

In an instant the blackness was spreading through the great cathedral city. Ships—small, commercial, and private machines—began to appear. But they hung outside the great cloud that spread, and finally were forced to stand motionless. Only a few foolhardy Tefflans dived through the cloud, as Aarn and Spence started out. The powerful magnetic bombs of the little spy ships brought down dozens of the attacking machines, but, as they reached the entrance, they saw a solid plug of a dozen ships in their path, with every evidence of staying there.

A dozen bombs—and the flaming wreckage dropped. Again the momentum drive lashed the engines on to full speed, and they leaped up the shaft.

"There'll be a destroyer outside," said Aarn's voice cheerfully through the communicating radios. "He won't be waiting for us—he'll have his destructive beam on us already. Our only chance is to pray he isn't directly in line with the opening, and dive out faster than light."

Spencer saw the rock of the opening running slowly away in slow dust as Aarn's words reached him—he threw his switch, and the tunnel mouth seemed to leap nearer. A great black shape loomed huge as they shot outward, a shape that was within inches of them. A cloud of hazy blue light leaped from Aarn's spy ship as he passed—Spencer saw it float slowly toward the bulk of the machine. Carlisle, seconds later, saw it eat into the destroyer and leave a great gaping hole in the armor.

Two little spy ships raced out for Teff-el faster than the message to hunt them could follow.

CHAPTER XIV

AARN LOOKED UP SLOWLY from the careful translation the Magyan scientists handed him. "I need more time to study this," he said at length, "for even your translation is not yet too clear to me, but I can say definitely that I can get through to that other space—my own home—by means of this diagramatic data."

"That is good news. Both to us, and to you, for it means that we shall again be able to visit the ancient world, the world where our race was born," said Anto Rayl. "I hope we shall be welcome."

"You will, Anto Rayl, you will be more than welcome. For the first century of our contact, your people will be mobbed by the anthropologists, philologists and most other ologists in the solar system.

"We will want to know as much about your race, as you will want to know about ours, and about the world from which you came."

Anto Rayl smiled. "For many years," he said "the scientists of our people were greatly puzzled. There were a great many races of animals in this world—most of which have been killed off in the battle between our people and the Tefflans, along with most of the large forms of vegetation—and none of these animals resembled our own race, yet all showed distinct traces of linkage. There was evolution among the various animal races, but no evolution that connected them with us.

"Not until—the ancient myths of the Ma-jhay-anhy and the Teff-hellani were so abundantly proved did the answer appear."

"It must have puzzled them," chuckled Spencer. "The scientists on our own planet, where all evolutionary strains were evident, had enough trouble convincing the bulk of the hide-bound people of the facts. You see, there was an ancient book, written by a race called the Jews, and this book was originally a sort of history of the race, half myth, half fact. As a mythological history it was well worthy of study, but it contained a parable of creation which every one had taken literally, for ages.

"Result: When science found the true story of creation written in the rocks, they could not convince the people who insisted the book was right."

"Man is a strange animal!"

"We have a religion, largely for those who want some higher power to believe in. Ma-ritha—the Lord of Life and Light. He was born of the Rocks of Earth, long ages before we came to this space, and for him our ancient land was named. He—"

Aarn had started at the name of the Magyan god. "Mithral The name's a good bit different—but, Anto Rayl, he was born of the Rock, and tended by the shepherds, who adored him, and gave him gifts—"

"Then the story of Ma-ritha survived?"

"Yes—complete," replied Spencer; "even to his wrestling with the Sun."

"And speaking of Sun," interrupted Aarn, "let us consider the progress on the sunbeam. Have you got any reports on the beams, Anto Rayl?"

"Yes; the tapping beam has reached the Sun, and the energy flood is on its way back now. It will reach us in about ten days more. It has made great progress while you were seeking the Ancient Tablets."

"It has. How about the installations on Ma-kanee and Ma-ran?"

"We've finished the borings, and we have started installing the great supplies of power coils. But we have been rather waiting a conference with you."

"I'll help you all I can, you know, Anto Rayl. What is it?"

"The Council of Warfare would like to discuss it with you. They have been preparing for this discussion, and will meet you in two hours."

"We will be there, Anto Rayl."

———◇———

Two hours later Aarn, Carlisle, and Spencer entered the great council room. The cavern was carved from a dark red rock, and lights of soft, amber glow flooded walls and ceiling, reflected in soft shadowless illumination, enriched by blue decorations of twisting gas-glow tubes about the ceiling till the natural sunlight effect of Anrel was attained.

A great table of richly carved, red gold occupied the center of the room. Gold, an ash, was common stuff to these men, useless save for decoration on planets where weight did not matter.

The Magyans were seated at the table, and Anto Rayl stood at attention beside the gray-haired, powerful figure at the head.

"These are the Strangers!" announced Anto Rayl ceremoniously.

"Let the Strangers enter," said Andar Minot, the chief of council.

"The Strangers within thy cavern accept the invitation with thankfulness at heart," Aarn's deep voice replied. "We bring with us what help we can. We offer what aid is within the power of our limbs and our minds."

"Be seated, friends," said Andar Minot, rising, the ceremonial greeting over. "We have called on you again. Our plans are more exact, and an exact plan requires an exact answer.

"First: By careful measurement of effects of known forces, we have been able to determine with accuracy the mass of each of our moons. We now know with exactitude the load that the driving engines must move.

"Second: astronomers have been observing and calculating, and the plan is made exactly according to their results. The smaller of our missiles, Ma-ran, will be used first. This will be torn from its orbit at a time when it is advantageously situated, and the acceleration of its orbital velocity will tear it loose in the exact direction we wish. It will then be projected—"

Carefully the plan was discussed, and the movements of each of the moons considered. Ma-ran would be equipped with a huge driving engine that would tear it loose from its orbit, to hurl down on Teff-el and Teff-ran, and the orbital forts. Ma-ran, though far lighter than Ma-kanee, would have a driving engine of equal power, because it would be expected to be mobile and capable of real motion, and be forced to pursue and catch the not entirely helpless orbital forts.

Ma-kanee, on the other hand, would merely hurl its quintillions of tons of mass on the planet—

The plan was made, and the work well under way. That same day Aarn and Spencer went out to Ma-kanee where the work was being done.

The little scout ship they were taken out on settled down near a great, arching glass dome, supported by heavy metal arches and braces. This had been an observatory for nearly six hundred years, actually, but now the instruments had been dismantled, and the records carried to the two moons which would remain here. This loss of two moons would be a serious thing to Magya. They had used these moons both as forts and as observatories. They had permitted many experiments under varying gravitational strains. And they had made possible many things that would no longer be possible.

Further, the stresses of tides would be suddenly relaxed, and despite their careful choice of locations for cavern cities, this was always a terrible danger, since Magya-quakes might result that would shatter the roof of some cavern and release thousands of tons of rock. The moons would, however, spiral away through several revolutions of the planet, so the strains might adjust themselves gradually.

Here, on the moon, the various organizations of mines, observatories, shipyards, and industries had been hastily shifted to the other moons. Ma-ran was small, and rather unimportant, but Ma-kanee was larger, and had been the seat of one of the greatest shipyards. This shipyard was now engaged in making the engines that would pull the satellite from the mother world. When this task was done, the apparatus would be transferred to the planet, and salvaged as far as possible.

—◇—

Beside the glass dome on Ma-ran was a great, dark tunnel leading to the bowels of the satellite. The surface structures had been possible for the same reason that battleships were possible—they were so dangerous they need fear no Tefflan ships.

No subterranean workings had existed. But now the tunnel led far below, and the scout ship slipped into it. Ten miles down, the tunnel was broken by a great air lock. The side of the great lock that plugged the entire enormous channel was a smaller lock, and to this their guide piloted his small ship.

"The large one is for the heavy freighters, carrying supplies. Takes power to pump all the air they need in locking. We use the back door." He smiled.

"What type of freighters have you? They weren't needed before. Did you use battleships for the task?" asked Spencer.

"Supply ships. We always had freighters. They were the heavy-load ships. They had to keep the fighters supplied when away from home. Remember they were filled with sun-power coils when you showed us how, but now this work has been going on, most of them have been taken apart, and the supplies of sun-power coils placed in these workings. We are making about one hundred large-size coils a day."

"And you need fifty thousand!" exclaimed Spencer. "Take a while yet, won't it?"

"Yes, but the capacity is being increased right along," the Magyan reminded him.

"How in blazes will they charge all those coils?" asked Carlisle. "They can't carry them back and forth to the Sun for power."

"Right. That's the whyfor of the Sun-tapping beam they set up way back yonder. The thing has been running about ninety days now, and the power will be on hand soon. They have it set to pull in plenty—thanks to Aarn's advice. He told them it was easier to throw away extra power than to get along without power you needed. They can just tap the Sun-tapping beam from here and charge their coils all they want."

"They can tap the tapping beam? But what happens if they draw more power than the beam is bringing, and then when they get through, the beam brings as much power as they drew. I mean, if they draw too much power, more than the beam is carrying, and then don't draw enough power, and—oh, Lord, what happens, anyway?"

Aarn and Spencer burst out laughing, as Carlisle stopped in confusion.

"What happens if you drink more water than there is in the glass, and then when there is enough water, don't drink it?"

"But you can't drink more water than there is then—"

"We can't get more power than is coming. Right. Second, the signal for more power will go down the beam, but they can always use power, so we aren't worried about that."

The lock gate ahead of them opened, and the little ship went on into the depths of the moon, in atmosphere now, for air had been released in the huge excavation.

"What did they do with all the rock?" asked Carlisle at length.

"Planted it all over the surface of the planet—satellite rather—so they wouldn't lose any weight. They want all they can get to smash down on the Tefflans."

Suddenly the dimly lighted, rough sides of the tunnel spread out into a brightly lighted cavern of huge size. A vast crew of men were laboring here, with machines of every description to aid them. The strange, screaming roar of Shal torpedoes was screeching at the rock, and the rock came cascading down in fine dust, to be caught in great vacuum machines and filtered out of the air instantly.

The caught dust was put in cartridges, and a pneumatic tube shot it up against the light gravity of the satellite and into the dome above, where the cartridge was emptied, the dust thrown outside, and the empty cartridge returned.

———◦◦◦———

On one side of the cavern, great metal frames had been constructed, and already ranks and ranks of huge antigravity coils were set up.

"Those are charged," explained their guide. "They were taken from the supply ships which are acting as freighters, and are supplying the power for the works here, now. Lights, power, machinery—everything."

The cavern was being expanded in two dimensions, the floor and the ceiling already determined. Artificial gravity plates had been installed in the place to make work easier, but the gravity had been reduced to only one-half normal for Magyans. The men, trained, soldier-mechanicians every one of them, were working under the commands of their officers, and rapidly setting up new racks of power machinery. Huge converters for the strange momentum oscillators were going in now. Bank after bank of oscillators.

"We have to drive conductors for miles through the rock in every direction to make certain we'd get perfect distribution of the momentum waves. That's the only reason we can move these moons, of course. If we'd had to depend on the space-drive disks, it would have been impossible. Just torn the thing to pieces."

Here and there they could see dark tunnels still unfilled, borings where Shal torpedo after Shal torpedo had burrowed its way on and on. The borings were less than six inches in diameter and hollow rods of aluminum had been thrust deep into them, to spread the momentum waves through the planetoid.

The great control-board panels were slowly assuming shape in the major control room. "We'll have six television stations on the surface, so arranged that we can see in every direction from in here. And we hope that you, Dr. Munro, will pilot Ma-ran in its flight on Teff-el!"

"If it is the will of the Council on Warfare, I would be glad to handle such a ship as this will be! A ship a hundred miles in diameter, weighing quadrillions and hundreds of quadrillions of tons!"

"Teff-el is as surely doomed as though Ma-ran were upon her now!" the Magyan exclaimed, a fire in his eyes that glowed at them in triumph. "At last this long battle our race has fought with the Tefflan race will be ended—through your aid!"

"I don't like to be—what my people sometimes call a crapehanger—but Teff-el was to have been crushed by the new ships equipped with the transpon beam and the magnetic and gravity bombs. She was not as thoroughly crushed as you and I expected. So never count Teff-el destroyed till her fragments hang before your eyes and clink against your ship."

"But nothing can withstand these incredible missiles! No energy could stop them."

"None that I can imagine. It is beyond the power of anything we know, certainly, but I would have said that a beam capable of disintegrating the armor of a mighty battleship was beyond the Tefflans' ingenuity. But—they destroyed battleships."

"But to stop such masses as these, they would first need something against which their momentum could be spent and—"

"Why stop them? Why not see to it they did not stop—let them miss Teff-el, and we could not again work the trick in our lifetimes. Could we let them circle Anrel and strike again on the circuit, we might feel safer. Suppose they have some driving engine capable of turning these worlds aside?"

"Ay—there is a possibility—but I do not believe it," the Magyan concluded smilingly.

"How soon will you be finished with this work?" asked Carlisle.

"It will take us about seventy days more at our present rate of progress. The great delay, of course, is in getting sufficient storage of power. Our sunbeam won't bring us power rapidly enough, and we will want to have the greatest possible velocity when we finish our work. Of course Ma-kanee will do most of the destructive work to Teff-el, but we must do our equally important share, and the fleet will have its great work. The Tefflans will be desperate. They will be very dangerous and fight with utter abandon."

On Ma-kanee, which they visited next, the work had not progressed as far, since a great deal of work had been needed in driving the three-hundred-and-fifty mile tunnel to the center of the sphere, and here, further, they found a metallic core. This was rather a help than a hindrance in some respects, however, for the tons and tons of metal were torn out of the center of the world with tremendous rejoicing.

"The fact is," explained their guide, "we have begun to plan on driving similar tunnels to the center of each of our other moons, if we find it possible. They are both totally devoid of natural heat. For some reason we had never thought of the possibility of getting the nickel-steel cores of the moons as a source of ready-refined armor plates!"

"Why stop with the moons? What's the matter with Magya itself?" asked Carlisle.

Spencer grinned and looked at Aarn.

Aarn answered: "It is possible on these moons because their gravities are low. I don't believe they will be able to do the trick with Ma-las. That's moon number two. That has a diameter of about one thousand miles and is so heavy that the surface gravity is really respectable. The result being, that before they reach the center of the planet, the weight of the superincumbent layers is so great per square inch that any metal, any substance there could be, is pressed into a sort of tarry state. Not liquid, but not solid. The pressure makes it run. The result is that it's impossible to drill a tunnel.

"On Magya, that condition is reached before you have gone ten miles down, to all practical intents and purposes. They couldn't tunnel deeper than that. If the metal core reached clear out there, they could go another half before it gave way, but rock, which composes that outer layer, yields.

"So they can't get the metal core of the planet."

"Nice cheap way to get armor plate!" Carlisle laughed. "Comes already alloyed, and all you have to do is saw out slabs."

"Don't you believe it! It has to be heat-treated for just one of many things. But the main thing is that the cost of drilling that tunnel is preposterous. The initial cost is so great that only the enormous amount of metal available can make it pay."

"Hmmm—that does make a difference. But, just the same, if they cut out much of that metal, Magya won't have to worry about battleship plate for centuries to come!"

"They don't intend to. That metal represents the main ballast of their deadly missile. They have to use it not as armor plate, but as an armor-piercing projectile."

Aarn gazed around the dim, raw cut that was rapidly being converted to a work camp in the heart of the little world. The hard metal was yielding slowly to the combined efforts of great transpon beams and friction saws. The saws had edges of a tungsten carbide alloy and were driven by compressed air. They had a speed of revolution in the near neighborhood of 60,000 r.p.m., and a velocity at the circumference approaching two miles a second. They had no teeth, but the sheer, wearing friction cut through the metal as if it was so much cheese.

A huge plug was sawn around, a plug some ten feet in diameter, and three feet thick. It was then fused out, and run into crucibles, promptly tapped into ingot molds, and shipped to the surface. There were some molds set up here, and the metal was being run into them to make various parts for the apparatus which would be needed, mainly frames to support coils and panels, and great tie-beds for the momentum apparatus.

Lights were still being strung, and as yet no great supply of coils had been moved in. Only one small frame, for there was scarcely room for more.

They returned to Magya, and Aarn set to work on his necessary calculations. Days passed in which they scarcely saw him, for, though they could sometimes help, in the main Aarn had retired into one of his silences. The old fellow who had calculated and observed had left his data in a form not too readily understandable to outsiders.

Perhaps he had not realized how many steps he was leaving out, since all was so plainly clear to him after the lifetime he had spent in gathering all the data. At any rate, many things had to be rechecked by Aarn, both for that reason, and to assure himself that certain figures were still good after the lapse of more than thirty thousand years of Earth-time.

In every case Aarn found the figures exact and still good.

He left his study occasionally—once to see the great sunbeam come in. The mighty star was sending back its flood of power now, after nearly one hundred and twenty days. There were, however, tremendous tides in the power, for Anrel was, as stated, a Cephid variable, and the luminosity and power of the giant sun varied continuously. But steadily the power was pouring into the huge banks of coils in the heart of Ma-ran. The coil banks here were completed and filled before the coil banks in Ma-kanee were ready to absorb, then they took the drain. Part, of course, was used by the battleships and scout ships that continuously patrolled space, defending the planet and its satellites against attack.

And, down near Teff-el, a fleet, a powerful fleet, was maintained in the disgust and terror of the city. Time and again the seeking, prying investigators, having pried out some secret of Teff-el appeared suddenly, only to explode destroying valuable works.

The great central power plant at Katakataml had been wrecked by a dozen investigators, exploded simultaneously, and the tremendous concussion of the exploding mercury boiler had brought down the cavern. The atomic fires that had burned in the checking, controlling generators were released, and Katakataml became a complete wreck. A new fleet base was needed.

But the watch of the Tefflans became more and more strict. The important secret places were carefully sealed so that it was impossible to get in, and then carefully searched that they might be certain that none had already been secreted.

But the cities were still open to the investigators, and suddenly the Magyan watchers noticed a rapidly growing feeling of relief and joy. There was a secret abroad; the Tefflans knew that a new invention had been made toward their cause. But they did not know what. Only those in charge knew, and they did not give it out.

"They say," said one Tefflan merchantship commander to a fleet officer, "that this new thing will wipe out Magya—every damnable monstrosity on the planet; that the last sacrifice to Kak-ka was directly responsible."

"Ay—ehuu—it was a sad day for us, that last sacrifice. Malee Faaing, the daughter of Leean Taol, was chosen, and old Leean Taol went near mad at the thought. And then he heard that Magyans were sighted in the Temple—a raid. He was in Kakkakill with his daughter, of course, and he hastened to the capture—and was baffled in the black cloud. He saw the golden gate, though, how the Magyan giant had sprung the bars like bits of wire—my faith, what strength the animal had—and he cursed.

"He cursed all the gods, and all men, and particularly all Magyans. Then some bumptious fool in the guard, hearing him, cursed him. He called him a fool of a chemist, a brainless old doddering wreck, and told him that the Magyan chemists had discovered a cloud of blackness combined with the very air to hide them. Why couldn't he find something that would kill the Magyans?

"And Leean Taol watched the sacrifice—of his daughter—and he partook of the sacrament—and he swore by Kak-ka and all the gods and the flesh and blood of that sacrifice that he'd end the struggle. And the rulers say he has!"

But what it was that the Tefflan chemist had discovered, no Tefflan knew, and no Magyan found out.

CHAPTER XV

"I CAN'T IMAGINE WHAT they have." Aarn sighed. "Apparently it's chemical. I hope it takes them a long time to make it. If it takes more than about eighty days more, we'll be getting back home, and their little planet will just be a ring of asteroids."

"But I don't see how they can do—what the only hint we have claims. They said they'd take the air away from Magya. That's an obvious impossibility. The mass is so great that no possible chemical combustive agent they can have could combine with it.

"How's your work getting on?" Spencer added, seemingly irrelevantly.

"Done!" Aarn sighed with contentment. "I have the apparatus ordered, and the Magyans can make it with Canning's help. You saw the final result."

"Uhmmm—but you didn't test it."

"You brainless meteor, how could I? I could test it by going home, which I am not prepared to do. I want to see the rest of this fight. I want to pilot Ma-ran as she crashes down on Teff-el. I want to wipe out that race which has been mankind's personification of evil since time began. I want to see this thing—"

Anto Rayl's feet sounded in the hall outside, his breath coming in gasps. "Aarn—Aarn—they've started! Their weapon—it's fire. It's started on the night side—weird fire—it burns blue—come—"

The three Solarians were on their feet already, racing for the ports of the *Sunbeam*. In seconds Canning joined them and Martin.

Out of the city in an instant—behind a thousand little fleeting scout and spy ships.

"The fleet—Tefflan fleet—sneaked out somehow—got out into space, and came within about ten million miles of Magya before they were detected. Hundreds of oversize scout ships. They dropped thousands and thousands of bombs. They were going slowly then of course.

"The bombs dropped to the planet. Painted black—on the night side—they have been discovered only now. The fleet chased the Tefflan fleet away, and they thought that no damage had been done till the bombs began to land," Anto Rayl explained rapidly.

Around the world from the afternoon side where they were to the night side they raced. It was a weird sight that met them. Enormous tongues of flame that stretched shimmering and pale-blue a hundred miles into the stratosphere, pale, blue, wavering light. They marched and countermarched, they rose and fell, and always sank.

They started here and there. And they ended always on the ground. But flame, burning hot flames that were still mingled with the blue flame, and tinged, under powerful lights, with brown smoke. A dozen, darting, black silhouettes shot through the flames.

"Spy ships."

Aarn tuned in the radio. A Magyan's voice sounded sharp—

"The temperature of the flames is so low they would not burn human flesh. But the chemical activity is strange. The flames on the ground are exceedingly hot, the ground itself is becoming incandescent. The vapors given off are foul and poisonous. They are red-brown in color—"

"Great God in heaven! The catalyst!" Carlisle almost shrieked it. "Magya's doomed as sure as Teff-el if we can't stop that! It's the catalyst—the catalyst—don't you fools see—the nitrogen catalyst—the atmosphere here is sixty per cent nitrogen—twenty-one per cent oxygen—they've found the catalyst and the whole atmosphere of the planet is burning to foul, poisonous, burning nitro-compounds! The whole atmosphere is going—the catalyst is never used, and the atmosphere is burning itself away!"

Anto Rayl had gone pale; Aarn was looking pale, too.

"Certain?" he asked sharply.

"What else?" snapped Carlisle. "Tell them to get samples—even if it costs lives. There's only one hope we can have. Only one way we can stop it, if—"

"Attention—attention all Magyan scouts and spies—" Anto Rayl had snatched the microphone from Aarn's hand. "Anto Rayl, C-8-N32 speaking—commander in chief of spies and scouts speaking. Listen, and all government forces listen: Carlisle, chemist of the Other Space, says this is a catalyst which causes oxygen and nitrogen to combine, burning up oxygen of the atmosphere. Deadly to us if not stopped. Get a sample. He needs it. Get enough for all chemists to work on. That is an order—C-8-N32 speaking."

Anto Rayl returned to the Solarians a bit sheepishly. "I am sorry I have not told you. Naturally we watched at first. Then I did not wish to say. It is by my orders that you have seen so much lately—taken everywhere. I am the commander of all minor ships. Unlike your navies, we have a horizontal as well as a vertical command. It makes for closer unity of action. I am under the command of the Commander of the Council of Warfare only. I investigated your ship when it first appeared because we, too, saw the strange materialization and your defense.

"Now forgive me, Carlisle, if it is within your power, save us—this other-space branch of your own race."

The weird, blue flames leaped high, while on the ground they continued to glow, mingled with the brown fumes and the red flare of normal burning.

Carlisle spoke rapidly: "The impossible catalyst. We've been looking for it for a century and a half. You see, nitrogen has one exothermic compound with oxygen—N_2O_5. That gives off heat in forming. Very little, comparatively, but some. That's why the flames were cold. N_2O_5 is the basis of nitric acid. It is a terrible oxidizing agent. All the organic matter in the soil is burning.

"We want it because, controlled, it would generate free power from the air, and, more important, manufacture fixed nitrates for, literally, less than nothing at all. Uncontrolled, it is burning the precious oxygen and the nitrogen to form the deadly, corrosive nitric compounds.

"Every particle of organic matter will be attacked. It will dissolve in the oceans and poison every species of creature. It will burn the air till there is no air, and sucks it out of your cities and leaves the people poisoned, and gasping. The oxygen will go, and with the nitrogen, to such a little volume the air pressure will fall, and then, no amount of locks will save your cities forever—"

"Any luck?" asked Aarn, looking at Carlisle.

The air in this room was very good, a little rich in oxygen. They were trying to help Carlisle all they could. In an air-tight retort, Carlisle had a sample of the deadly stuff. He looked up at Aarn's entrance. His face was pale, and haggard, his eyes tired.

"Better take a rest, Carlisle," said Aarn.

"No luck. Can't analyze it. Hasn't a chemical formula. Can't rest—the air pressure has fallen so now they can't keep up the pressure inside. That's only twenty days of it. And we can't stop it. We've *got* to stop it."

"Know it. But you won't stop it being tired. Knock off for a while."

"Say, Aarn, why don't they fix the locks here? They say they can't keep up the air pressure because the locks leak so. But they don't fix them. I thought they were proof against gases. Designed to keep poisonous gases out, and guaranteed gas-tight."

"Uh—in the usual way," snorted Aarn. "They kept the poisonous gas out by pushing the good air out faster than it could come in. Result—they never planned on this. Then, too, it wouldn't do a bit of good to fix the locks, and rocks leak."

"Rocks leak?"

"Certainly! Full of cracks that they never worried about. Porous, so that it can seep through. With a pressure difference of nearly ten pounds to the square inch, that means leakage. And they can't suck it in fast enough to keep it up. Men not on active duty are being kept asleep as much as possible. Use less air."

"Why can't they suck enough air in—build larger filters."

"Time. They can't build them in time. They've started, of course. But, you see, they have to be proof against those ultra-microscopic particles. The worst of it is that it isn't the solid stuff that's doing the damage. Remember how terrible the gases were when they started the things—and the filters didn't get out the fine stuff.

"It killed thousands—we missed the worst of it in the *Sunbeam*. In the civilian cities it was worse because they didn't have ships to retire to while adjustments were made. The filters would easily handle this—if they didn't have to be nearly choked off to stop the fine stuff."

"I can't analyze this. I haven't found a poison for the catalyst. And I can't see any other way out. The rest of the chemists here are as helpless as I am."

Carlisle turned wearily back to his work, and Aarn went out. He got into a little scout ship and was let out through a very small lock. In the twenty days that had passed, Magya had changed. The whole world was blanketed under a pall of white snow. But the snow was slushy and about two feet deep.

It glowed blue, and the air glowed with a dim blue haze, and a constant rain of white crystals that fluttered gently down added to the slush. There were no more red flames of burning organic material. That was all burned away long since. The air was full of the floating particles of the catalyst dust. The ground was covered with it. The water was full of it.

Thick, oily brooklets of thick nitric acid boiled and fumed brown as they crept down to the sea, bearing their load of undissolved, solid nitric pentoxide. The streams hissed and boiled water and brown vapor as they met the sea and dissolved. The air outside, could it have been smelled by any living creature, was a burning, terrible poison. Billions of tons of atmosphere had already been burned away.

The burning was slower now, for each pound of nitrogen had carried down with it three pounds of oxygen, and the atmosphere was almost nothing but nitrogen and carbon dioxide. There was no water in the air, for the nitric oxide absorbed it, drank it greedily. The carbon dioxide was formed from every scrap of organic matter that had been on the planet.

There were no fish in the sea, no plant nor any animal on the land, and no bird in the air. The humus in the soil was burned; the very rocks were being eaten by the corrosive, oily stuff.

The nights were cold now, and the thick rivulets froze. The days were hot, and the snow melted under Anrel's rays and ran into the sea, liquid itself. The sea was an ocean of strong nitric acid. The very spy ship Aarn rode was being eaten slowly by the corrosive gas, and a trail of light brown fumes floated out behind.

Out on Magya's four moons there was a deadly activity. Men were working with the grim determination that Teff-el should die, even as Magya perished, for there was little hope. Even if the catalyst stopped now, they feared the end would be inevitable.

The air glowed blue, night and day. The great, clear stars of this space were invisible, for the light in the air hid them.

Aarn settled to the planet and opened a little trap. It closed, and as the ship rose, there was a mass of nitric oxide in it. A moment later he had taken a similar sample from the water of the nitric-acid sea. Then he rose, and at an altitude of ten thousand feet took a sample of the thin air.

Later, back in the city, Carlisle made a hurried test of the various samples. The catalyst, still active, was in the air, in the snow, and in the ocean. It was everywhere.

"They're still rejoicing on Teff-el," snapped Carlisle. "Spencer was in a while ago and said that Teff-el has at last made investigators, and there were some flying around on the planet recently. They're watching with glee."

Aarn's grin deepened. "Wait till they send investigators out to the moons."

"They have," snapped Carlisle. "They're examining the works carefully, I suppose."

"Oh, no, they aren't. They're discovering that the Magyans are preparing to move to the moons."

"They'll send the damnable catalyst there," groaned Carlisle.

"Much good it may do them. They probably have got the catalyst in there before this. But—they've changed the air in the moons to pure oxygen at reduced pressure. The catalyst can't find any pure nitrogen to work on."

Aarn had slipped up behind Carlisle, and now he deftly slipped an arm about his friend, lifted him up and away from his bench, and as Carlisle opened his mouth in protest, Aarn popped a pill in it, and simultaneously grabbed his nose.

"Whoa—kiddie. Swallow nasty medicine like good little boy. Baby boy's gotta sleep, or he'll go clean off his orbit."

Perforce, Carlisle choked, and swallowed.

"Just a bit of your own pet diamorph. Give you a nice heavy sleep for twenty hours that you wouldn't take. Ah—baby's quieting down."

Carlisle wasn't—but Aarn's arms were quieting him. Carlisle was as helpless as any baby might have been, save that a child, being possessed of unlimited flexibility in his joints, can become incredibly hard to hold, and Carlisle couldn't. Aarn took him to his room aboard the *Sunbeam* and put him on the bunk.

"You might as well stay there now, Trolley Car, because I won't let you out, and you are just naturally bound to go to sleep pretty quick, anyway."

"I've got an antidote for this stuff," Carlisle snapped angrily. "You interfering half-witted physicist, I've got to find that catalyst poison."

"You moronic, subnormal idiot, you can't go without sleep indefinitely. You passed out twice in an experiment, so I'm just stopping you ahead of time this time—and you'll sleep. Nighty-night, you asteroid."

Aarn left. With a groan of utter, irresistible weariness Carlisle sank back into his bunk, and instantly was asleep.

Aarn went down to the control room, and sat thinking. Aarn was not a chemist; he was a physicist, but like any scientist, he knew something of almost all others. He tried to recall what he knew of nitrogen, of oxygen, of their mutual behavior.

With a start he sat up, and finally got Carlisle's notes. "He writes a misbegotten sort of a hand," he said disgustedly, looking at the sloppy notes.

The book was spotted with everything imaginable, and in many places there were irregular holes that grew when looked at, the paper was so rotted by acids and bases.

Aarn sat down and at last came to what he wanted. A spectral analysis of the catalyst. Simple—thus far. But how were those elements combined?

He looked at the list of them. And one he had rather hoped to see was there—titanium. With a sigh, he settled deeper and considered. Titanium, he remembered, was one of the few elements which burned readily in nitrogen; also oxygen. Perhaps that was the active principle.

If he could just find some substance that would combine with the titanium permanently—he'd suggest that to Carlisle when he woke up, anyway.

Spencer appeared presently, looking tired. "Been working out on Ma-ran. They're pushing the work. They have it almost all finished. Final plans called for an engine as powerful as the driving mechanism of Ma-kanee, but they've made it bigger. The air here's getting pretty bad. I hear they can't get oxygen. Why can't they take that damnable residue outside and break it down?"

"The catalyst," said Aarn with a gentle sigh. "That, like the famous French phrase of the 1915's 'c'est la guerre', is the answer to all questions here, at present. They can't get the catalyst out of the snow or the liquid, and if they try to break it up, it just goes right back together, and the catalyst tends to escape into the air of the room—and that's why they don't do it."

"Any hope, Aarn?"

"Uhmm—if they smash those moons into Teff-el soon enough. Then we might move to some other planet—at least a lot of them could. Not all—but a lot. Might save the race, at least. Before Teff-el is smashed, the Tefflans would kill the new colony."

"The moons will move in fifty days, smash Teff-el in sixty three."

"The council says the population will be small enough to move into the warships in thirty at the present rate."

CHAPTER XVI

"THAT IDEA IS INTERESTING—YOU have a notion it acts something like the haemoglobin in the blood, then—carries combined nitrogen to oxygen, is freed of the nitrogen by the oxygen, and, immediately goes back for more nitrogen in some way?" Carlisle seemed to turn the idea over in his mind. "Interesting thought—but the thing is, titanium wouldn't do that—it's just against all chemistry."

"Uhmmmm—so's this blinkin' catalyst. You haven't made any better suggestions, I take it. Now what would stop it, if that's the case? You know—something like carbon monoxide in the blood. Combines with the haemoglobin and stays that way."

"The chloride is a liquid. And peculiarly stable. The fluoride is a solid—I've tried all those things—all the gases I could think of."

"Well, try some more. Try something like ClO_2—a compound of chlorine for instance, with oxygen, so while the oxygen of the compound grabs the nitrogen, the chlorine can slip in."

"This isn't a game of puss in the corner," objected Carlisle. "But I get your idea—I think I'll try something on that idea. But it will have to be an oxy-compound, because nothing else can exist—out there!"

"How goes it now?" asked Aarn, looking in once more at Carlisle's lab. "Any luck?"

"Shut up and keep out—I'm busy."

Aarn retired.

It was the twenty-third day when Carlisle came out. The air in the city was unbreathably thin. The oxygen content was so low that people were gasping for breath under the slightest exertion, while many of the old, those with weak heart or lungs, had already gone into eternal sleep.

But Aarn recognized Carlisle's joy as he came out. "I've got something—it worked a little—" It was a sealed glass tube, a peculiar greenish-yellow liquid that had the characteristic color of substances green by transmitted and yellow by reflected light. It was volatile, thin liquid, and Carlisle was volatile today.

"Come—look—" Aarn was already beside him. The laboratory door shut, and the air inside was noticeably richer, the oxygen content higher.

In the glass dome, there was a little pile of the deadly white nitrogen snow, and a steady blue glow, where oxygen and nitrogen fed into it. Carlisle broke the stem of his sealed tube, and a pungent, biting odor spread through the room. The liquid boiled instantly, and frost collected on the tube. Carlisle held it in a cloth now, as the gas was sucked into the bell jar.

Instantly the blue flame died, and went out. Carlisle resealed his tube in a flame, and no amount of shaking revived the catalyst action.

"I've heated it; I've separated the N_2O_5, and I've done everything else. The catalyst is dead—and stays that way!"

"Can we make that?" demanded Aarn.

"We've got to," answered Carlisle. "And we can. It takes—I don't know how little. It's the poison. It's a chlorine compound—you were right. My Lord, the thing—it's done! We—we can live here!"

"Shut up!" snapped Aarn. The man was nearly hysterical from the release of strain. "Get to work and teach the other chemists. We need tons of it—we've got to open those filters first—let the poisonous air come in, and take that catalyst out. Is the anticatalyst poisonous?"

"No—see." Carlisle took a deep breath of the fumes. "It's biting—acrid—a heavy dose might be, but only as hydrochloric acid is. It burns a bit, but in the low concentration. Send all the men up—I've got the poison!"

Hours later flasks of the stuff were coming out. A thin, volatile liquid. Chemists were regulating the flow into the great air filters of the city. In every city similar scenes were being witnessed. The catalyst was no longer deadly. The air could be sucked in more rapidly, the poisons eliminated.

Hours later still—great retorts set up—glass chambers with their loads of deadly snow were being cooked, and plentiful, rich air came out—

Three days—the gas was boiling out of great tanks now, being dropped from low-flying machines, and high-flying machines, and everywhere the catalyst sucked it in—and died.

The flame of deadly blue died, and the nitric oxide at last began to cease its constant fall. Little light flakes drifted down for days, as slow release of the catalyst poison found the last active trace of catalyst.

----◦◦◦----

Already, huge beam stations had been set up, and great sunbeams reached out to tap the main beam, and hour after hour, great fan arcs reached out across the ground, and the burning arcs caught the snow, converted it in an instant to vapor at thousands of degrees—and smashed the snow back to pure oxygen and nitrogen, the lesser oxides of nitrogen breaking down instantly in the arc. Other stations were being built by the sides of the lakes, by the oceans, at the mouths of rivers. The thick, oily rivers, loaded with the terrible, burning stuff flashed into clean, burning electric flame, and the nitric gases returned to the air as nitrogen and oxygen.

In the cities, life was easy once more, air plentiful, and the outside air pressure rapidly rising. It would be years, perhaps, before the last of the terrible nitric oxide was gone, before men could venture forth into—

Rains were falling again, now. After a brief three days the terrific arcs that boiled away seas and lakes and rivers were throwing rain clouds into the air, and rain began to wash the stuff in thick torrents to the sea, clearing the land rapidly.

The water was loaded with thousands of tons of soluble stuff. Landslides, even minor quakes, changed the topography as the terrific erosive actions became evident. In mere days, the erosion of centuries had taken place!

But it would be years before the soil was fit to bear again, centuries before the seas had been freed of their deadly load of acid. For, active as nitric acid is, and unstable as its compounds are, there were billions on billions of tons of it.

"It will be a generation," said Carlisle, "before the land will be fertile again. Then it will be superfertile, for the place is soaked in nitrates as no other land ever was. The Tefflans have solved the problem of nitrates for all time to come. By the way—when it no longer counted, I found a way to analyze that blamed stuff, and succeeded in making some. Did you hear what was done with it?"

"No, I've been busy with Spence, setting up arc stations to destroy the stuff."

"A load of it was dumped on Teff-el just on chance. They had the destructive catalyst, of course—they wouldn't have dared to use the thing as a weapon if they hadn't, and the scout brought back a sample of their anticatalyst. By the time he got it here it was just a mixture of elements. Their anticatalyst breaks down so rapidly it couldn't have been analyzed, if we had tried the trick sooner."

"I expected that, too," said Aarn. "I thought of dumping a load of the snow—infected snow I might call it—on Teff-el, to see what they'd do."

"Yes—so did I. But I realized that they'd either let the small amount we had go, or gather it up, and treat it privately. The one thing they couldn't do would be let to us get a sample of that anticatalyst."

"The work on the moons has been deserted temporarily, and our investigators on Teff-el report that their investigators on Magya report a cessation of the efforts to make the moons habitable to their people, so we aren't sorry. In other words, they really thought we were going to move to the moons. The cities will have to be kept closed because of the bad gases outside, anyway, so that there will be no trouble with their investigators getting in and reporting on how the people in our cities feel."

CHAPTER XVII

THE GREAT CUBICLE SPACE was huge, yet packed with apparatus. It was almost one thousand feet on a side, a billion cubic feet of space, yet the great storage coils banked up and away, solid, on all sides of the tiny control and living quarters in the lower corner of the room. The apparatus and labor expended in the construction of this great thing represented the equal of nearly 600,000,000 dollars. A similar enormous sum had been needed for the apparatus—and only part of the labor of constructing the huge power chamber in the heart of Ma-kanee. But nearly 100,000,000 dollars' worth of metal had been extracted, which made the cost of the two just about equal.

If this venture failed, Magya would be hard put for some time. Many necessary industries on the home planet had suffered from the men diverted here, but the nitric acid inundation had naturally been costly beyond estimation.

Aarn, Spencer, and Carlisle stood on a platform high among these great-heaped coil masses and looked down in wonder. "All charged?" asked Spencer at length.

"Filled completely," nodded Aarn. "Remember, the new power message went down to the Sun and back while we were working on this. By the time that flood got here, we had use for it, and it's been filling coils at the rate of two an hour, both here and on Ma-kanee. Both moons' coils are full."

"Really—the destructive energy that will blast—a full-sized planet—is concentrated now in those coils." Carlisle looked at the vast array of coils in something approaching horror. "What would happen if they all released their energy at once?"

"Volatilize this moon. Do the same for Ma-kanee, I guess," replied Aarn. "They won't, though. We took certain precautions, I assure you. Though they will be short-circuited at the last final plunge, when the moon strikes Teff-ran. Ma-kanee's coils will go when it strikes Teff-el. But you see, not only all the energy stored here—which is enough in itself—but also the energy of falling through five hundred million miles of Anrel's enormous gravitational field, plus the natural orbital velocities of both Magya system and the individual moon will aid Ma-kanee, our main weapon. Ma-ran here, will be slowed up, and under better control, because it has other duties to perform!"

A sudden, dull, humming note sounded twice. Carlisle started, and the other two stiffened. "First warning," said Aarn softly, relaxing. "That's the warning from the astronomers on Ma-kanee. They sent the first warning and they'll begin accelerating now, in about thirty-two and a half minutes. They're starting the oscillator tubes, warming them up."

Unconsciously, Aarn looked down. Two enormous glass tanks loomed thirty feet high, two tanks filled with metal plates, and huge heaters, grids and screens—the oscillator control tubes. Beside them loomed two cold tubes with a sprinkling of mercury over them, about ten feet high, and some five in diameter. They were the "chopper" tubes which were designated to chop the current off abruptly at an enormous frequency—

Again the two dull humming notes. "The choppers!" said Aarn softly. His eyes shifted to the great bulking lumps of the momentum drive itself. "That comes next—run direct current through them for a while to warm them. Then when they break that current the oscillation is started—"

Three notes. "Let's go below." Aarn led the way down. In the control room there was quiet confusion. Men were rapidly walking back and forth. Seven different radio positions were occupied. Three more television control positions, and, finally, the great panel where the main controls were, with the three television screens and the selector dials which would throw any part of space on the screen, or into any one of the telescopes.

A low, powerful throbbing hum sounded. As Aarn threw a switch, the television disk before him lighted up suddenly, as the beating note ceased, and the face of the controller on Ma-kanee appeared. His face was drawn and intent as he threw a switch. Suddenly an enormous cat began to whine, its whine mounted, and steadied to a great, gentle purr. Another—another—another—

"Gyroscopes," said Aarn. "They have to stop the spin of the moon first. They have small momentum controls that are controlled by the big gyroscopes. They'll hold it firm."

There was a steady, grumbling roar sounding now from the speaker. Ma-kanee was being stopped in her age-long rotation. Only slight disturbance was caused, because every particle was being decelerated, but there was a certain amount of oblateness, and this was flattening out, or rounding out, with groaning protest.

The controller started, and turned to someone behind and to one side of him. "All proceeding as directed. The main tubes and apparatus are warm now, ready for operation if necessary."

The man behind him made some inaudible answer, and the controller, Hirun Theralt, checked all the dials before him.

Quickly the time passed. All the men on Ma-kanee were busy, working frantically as the moment of the start approached. Finally the controller spoke directly into his microphone.

"To the Council of Astronomy: My rotation shows zero. Is this correct?"

A voice answered metallically from a concealed speaker. "That is correct. Read off your coördinates, and we will give you the correct axes."

"X-543-27. Y-732-45. Z-982.38."

"Set the controllers at: X-234-31, Y-135-52, Z-64-32. Let the master controls rest at this, and watch only your deviation axes readings. Keep these as directed in further messages. Are they now reading zero?"

"They are zero, and are holding. The automatic antirotation apparatus has been attached, and standardized."

"Continue as instructed, with acceleration along X at the rate of 752,000 units. At the second signal, increase to 1,435,000 units, and continue except as directed."

The controller repeated the instructions, his voice trembling a trifle.

Minutes dragged. Then finally came a soft buzz. Another, another— "At the tenth," said Aarn softly, "he will start—"

Eight—nine—ten— A groan echoed softly from the loudspeaker, and a great snarling vibration echoed instantly, and died in a shrillness. A blue light glowed down from above, where the great mercury tube boiled in sudden activity.

"Acceleration at seven-five-two," said the controller.

"That means," explained Aarn, "seven hundred and fifty thousand millions tons of force. They plan to increase it by steps—"

On the screen, a sudden blankness came, a shift, then the image of an elderly, gray-haired man. "The view we will send now, is a model map of the actual, and the correct theoretical position of Ma-kanee. This will show the deviation from her normal orbit."

The screen was black, save for a green circle, Magya, two red and blue dots. The dots were points on great ellipses. Slowly, slowly, they could see the red dot near Magya creeping along. The others seemed almost motionless.

Hours later, the inner red dot had made a complete circuit, and now there were three red dots, and two blue. Ma-kanee's dot had split in two. One of the Ma-kanee dots was slowly circling on a greater, and ever-growing orbit. More and more power was being applied. The slow acceleration was increasing gradually.

Again Ma-ran swung about in her orbit—and now Ma-kanee was hundreds and thousands of miles from her assigned orbit. She was struggling mightily now, with increasing momentum and centrifugal force to pull herself free of the bonds of Magya. Her orbit was lengthening more and more toward a straight line. She was on the night side of Magya now, soon she would fly off on the day side—and escape toward Anrel. Then the acceleration that was being applied would change in direction, change to bend the normal orbital speed about Anrel toward the sun, instead of at right angles. The centrifugal force no longer acting against it, Anrel's pull might drag the moon even faster toward Teff-el.

The screen was showing many different scenes now. At length it showed a scene that was relayed from a ship far away—a ship hanging off Teff-el! An investigator, one of those that still had not been found, was showing the streets of Cantak.

Teff-el had seen and understood, when Ma-kanee started her movement. Not fully understood, for they believed it only a great weapon—a great battleship that no battleship could fight. A battleship that would come down and ray them out of existence—destroy every ship, every orbital fort—and finally the forts on Teff-ran. Then Ma-kanee, they feared, would set up in an orbit about Teff-el, and never again would a Tefflan ship be able to reach the surface! Every city isolated—till tunnels could be dug to connect them!

There was panic, and excitement. Tremendous loads of supplies were being rushed out to Teff-ran, that she might defend the planet, perhaps conquer even the mobile moon!

Aarn smiled grimly. "Futile," he said. "Nothing could help. They might carry some of their people away—but the Magyan fleet is already waiting just off Teff-el. They can't get away. There are almost no ships near here."

"What if the Tefflans attack?" asked Carlisle.

Aarn lighted a cigarette carefully. There were few left now. "If they did, what would they attack? The moon? Much good that would do them. Magya? Where? How? There's nothing on the surface, and they couldn't reach the cities before our fleet could start in on one of their orbital forts, and start cleaning up thoroughly. They'd have to be called home."

It took days, and long before the process was finished, Tefflan ships of war were circling viciously off Ma-kanee—and occasionally there was a flash of instantaneous blue incandescence as the inconceivable coils of the moon ship were shorted by a mere cruiser.

But finally Ma-kanee sailed proudly free, and bent her orbit more and more toward Teff-el.

And then, one day, there was further stirring among Magya's children, and Teff-el was stricken by horrible panic.

Aarn, his iron nerves alone subduing the trembling that crept into them, pressed a series of controls. And huge oscillator tubes glowed dull-red. The power board sprang into life across the way, and Aarn read its warnings and its story, and returned to his own control board.

The tremendous transformers hummed suddenly and the great chopper tubes glowed green-blue, great arcs roared as tumbler switches snapped across. Then the shrill snarl of speeding gyroscopes. The enormous power plant that was Ma-ran, was waking to life. Huge cables that spread out like the threads of a three-dimensional spider web began to glow softly as a low power oscillated through them, and gently, but swiftly, the spin of Ma-ran was slowed. There were no observatories outside here. Ma-ran was to be far more active and far more destructive than her larger sister as she ran amuck.

On Ma-kanee, observatories had been dismounted. There were no more machines, no lenses—only the transpon-projectors that bit into the feeble attacking moths of the cruisers. The apparatus had been carried away, and already, as the great coils were exhausted in accelerating the ship that was a world, they were being recharged again. Then, when these were again discharged, the great supply ships would take them on. Before Ma-kanee finally struck Teff-el, it would be little more than a hollow moon. The machinery would be salvaged. But Ma-ran was to be an active deadly thing all her short life as a ship; there would be no salvaging of machinery here. Every coil was to be emptied not once, not twice, but four times.

And as the final signal came, Aarn was on his own. He had only a ship. Carefully he had worked out the course he wanted to follow, and now, with his enormous craft, he turned in the tremendous power. A shrill whine built up, the moon trembled and shattered with the fall of rocks outside, loose material suddenly sliding as the planetoid trembled, started—and moved!

CHAPTER XVIII

"WE'RE ON THE RIGHT course," sighed Aarn after checking his readings once more. "This ship isn't exactly responsive. But—good Lord, what power!" He looked up through the glass roof of the power room to the gigantic, glowing, platinum bars that represented the filament heaters of the oscillator tubes. Beyond rose tier on tier of great coils. Men were working among them now, weightless, for the gravity had been turned off. The coils, rapidly being shifted from one transpon beam set-up to the other, were being prepared for the first charging. A transpon beam would soon reach out across space to tap the great permanent beam structure that was now several million miles away. A recharge was needed. Ma-ran had just escaped the gravity of Magya.

Aarn looked through a tiny cross-hair instrument at an exceedingly sensitive and accurate television device—and saw he was exactly on his course, according to the stars of this space.

He straightened again, and flipped a televisor control. The screen before him swirled, and lighted up with the scene aboard the Ma-kanee. The controller on duty now was again Hirun Theralt. He looked up with a smile. "You are on course, and all is going well?"

"Perfectly. We are about 3,000,000 miles behind you now. We'll be passing in a few days. They been bothering you much?"

Hirun Theralt smiled woodenly. "Slightly," he acknowledged. "We have destroyed fifteen cruisers, ten destroyers—and scout ships by the score! They have stopped annoying. And you?"

"We aren't fighting at all—we found that the disintegrators can't get through all the rock and stuff. So we're just not noticing them. Several of them getting ready to land have been destroyed by a transpon beam, though. We forbid landing."

"They're taking out our coils. They've been discharged completely."

"Aye—I saw the supply ships coming. You have no control left?"

"We are maintaining control only by means of the battleships, remember."

"They won't salvage this apparatus," Aarn said rather sadly. "They can't really use the power plant anyway—nothing else this big to move."

Hirun Theralt laughed, and Aarn suddenly started, as he saw Anto Rayl appear in his screen, smiling, too. "Don't be so sure! We are thinking seriously of going after some of those minor planetoids out beyond there, and hauling them in whole for moons—and metal."

"Not too bad an idea—hi—two battleships!" Aarn started in surprise, as on his side screen, two Tefflan battleships appeared, suddenly swooping down. A faint tingling stirred in Aarn's flesh, a lethargy, that was yet mixed with a strong, tearing stimulus—

"The death ray!" he called in surprise. "They have power in that—" He was working swiftly. About him, as he sounded the alarm, a dozen other men had appeared as if by magic, and a tremendous activity of switches and power boards took place.

"Defense power in," snapped a young Magyan power lieutenant.

"Propulsive power doubled," another called, as he finished his work.

"Turn the sun-tapper beam up, for full drain available, and prepare to turn it into a waste beam if necessary," snapped Aarn, going to work. Even to this enormous thing, a battleship attacking with death-dance rays could be deadly.

The battleships came rapidly, swooping nearer. Aarn turned four huge transpon beams on the first ship, and, when he was sure his sighting devices had had time to keep them aligned, he sent out all the power they could safely carry.

One—two—three—they struck. An enormous, scintillating splotch of light exploded suddenly on the walls of the first battleship—it flared and grew to a terrible, blinding sun, a spot of light ten feet across, with a billion horse power pounding against it! But the wall of the ship did not yield! Aarn started in surprise—and at that moment the greater sun-tapping beam power came in. The spot of light spread like an eating acid, flared to an incredible temperature, the metal behind that light—

"They've stopped it," Aarn groaned. "A sheath of some sort of transpon condition. I knew they'd analyze it eventually."

"What does that mean?" snapped Spencer.

"The transpon beam is useless! They can—" As he spoke, the moon tingled with a terrific shock of the death beam.

Aarn turned his face up slowly, and it twitched with the shock of the beam,—"absorb power from us," he finished. He pulled a dozen switches, and the transpon beams died; only the coils drank in the power now. "Without that supply of power, they can't kill us with this mass of material in the way of their high frequency note."

Already from far across space, Magyan battleships were appearing. Here and there, a ship materialized suddenly from nothingness, slowing to speed less than that of light. Battleships racing to the call of the Ma-ran. The warning had gone out by radio—but on the surface of Ma-ran there were scout stations, where scout ships capable of exceeding light speed lay constantly ready. With the first sight of the battleships, they had started. Those who had remained on the outside of Ma-ran had died when the beam struck.

The Tefflan battleships turned, and with their terrible destructive beams started work on the Magyan fleet. Their beams were far more powerful, the center of their great ships hollow, letting the gravity bombs explode harmlessly. The magnetic bombs were useless against that thick metallic armor of the battleships—

And a Magyan battleship slowly, slowly crumbled away. Another began to drift helplessly, as the men within it died— Thermite bombs were glowing on the great sides of the battleship—and as they ate through, the Magyans saw within a three-foot layer of the red-gold. It carried away the thermite's heat so rapidly that no break was made.

"They came prepared," murmured Aarn gently. Spencer looked at him in wonder. Aarn had a plan, evidently. "But there are limits—limits in everything. Now I wonder—" Aarn grew busy with the televisor, making strange gargling noises, thinking carefully and painfully before each.

"Code," he said, as Spencer looked at him with troubled eyes. "Not a language. They know what I mean though when—"

Presently Aarn was setting up a great many beam circuits, and far across space a great many other men were working very hard. They were men on Ma-kanee, and on the supply ships, and elsewhere—

"Spence," said Aarn, "if you think you have seen heat, or seen power—just you reconsider."

Presently, Aarn was ready, and he growled and gargled something else. Ten seconds later, his eyes glued on a super-accurate chronometer, he pressed a button. Then he looked eagerly at the screen. Great transpon beams had reached out in three directions, and simultaneously, the whole great coil system of Ma-ran, the great tapping beam that was reaching out to the main tapping beam that extended from Magya to Anrel—all were in the circuit.

And, in the middle of space, close to the point where the two Tefflan ships fought end to end, it happened. The aiming was very accurate. The great power coils of the supply ship near Ma-kanee, the remaining power coils of Ma-kanee, the power coils of six Magyan battleships—all were pouring their power into a single beam. And the combined might of the tapping beam, and Ma-ran's coils against it!

Then, while the Magyan fleet retreated, a Magyan scout ship was started for that energy center—and reached it at just the moment it came into being. There were no men in the ship, and the ship flashed into instantaneous gas, and gas at such a temperature that the thermite had been cold by comparison. The molecules were split to atoms and the atoms smashed to electrons and protons and negatrons and neutrons—and they exploded outward with something approaching the speed of light. And the wasted energy became radiant energy, and anything anywhere near that energy center was heated by it.

Not the mild warmth of a thermite bomb—located in a spot—but the heat such as a minor sun might give. Billions of horse power. Not a heat ray, but a wild, uncontrolled heat center.

The Tefflans were suddenly glowing white at the end nearest the center. The heat spread, and even as the ships started, the rear sections slumped molten, and floated away, blazing white and blue in the heat of the center. The fore sections, no longer shadowed, unable to accelerate into a speed faster than light, and escape, as the nearer Magyan ships had, turned red, and smoked—

They fell easy prey to a few hundred gravity bombs, for the center of the ship was not the center of half the ship. And the transpon condition shield failed and the battleships became, in short seconds, flaming incandescent wreckage.

Slowly, the heat center died, as the conflicting powers were withdrawn gradually, lest some ship be injured by an unchecked beam.

Aarn smiled slightly at Spencer. "I hope they haven't any more like that. I hear that they destroyed seven of our ships before they got out here—"

"They haven't, I suspect, or they'd have sent them all. They were afraid of this moon."

CHAPTER XIX

"I THINK OUR COURSE will be X-235-89," Aarn said. His voice was low, and tense. Ma-kanee was thousands of miles behind now—but in the forward televisor disk, Teff-el showed a huge, round disk. And about the little moon, traveling now with a velocity of thousands of miles an hour, but slower now than Ma-kanee, a fleet of great battleships wove a constant pattern. An angry, threatening halo of destruction, strengthened and widened by the heavy cruisers, and light cruisers, and destroyers. Almost the entire navy was here, for Ma-kanee needed no protection now. Ma-kanee was deserted. There was no apparatus, save for two or three televisors, and a small crew of men to observe. Ma-kanee was a hollow hulk, seven hundred miles in diameter, driving down on a doomed world.

Teff-el was under no delusions now. They knew that Ma-kanee was not intended to capture forts, and their moon—they knew what it meant. And that was the reason for the heavy protection that was offered Ma-ran. The Tefflans knew that Ma-kanee had no driving engine, that they had no possible weapon capable of turning it. Their only hope lay in capturing Ma-ran, and using it to batter Ma-kanee aside.

The buzz saw of circling, deadly ships was not revolving unhindered. Scout ships of the Tefflan fleet kept darting in, hoping to launch an unsuspected torpedo, or some weapon which might pierce the magnetic and antigravity shields.

Then the thing happened which the Magyans had been expecting. The Tefflan commercial fleet swam up from their cities, formed with incredible speed, and swept out into space. They went directly away from the approaching moons, out from Teff-el in such a direction that the battleships of Magya would have to circle wide around the planet to attack them, for the great forts were in action. Instantly the fleet about Ma-ran split, according to previous orders. The newest, fastest ships disappeared in speed greater than light. On the other side of Teff-el, the fleet of thousands had split, scattered in every direction.

This was not merely a migration—it was an attempt at escape, an attempt filled with hatred, and bitterness—

"If only," said Miuut Kakin, "we can have but one shipload of the colonists safely through—safely on that planet Tieranl—they can establish a secret colony—we will yet have some chance of wiping out thousands of those misconceived Magyans!"

Miuut Kakin was in charge of the Tefflan escape. He himself would not go. He would die—with most of the planet's inhabitants.

And just about five thousand miles beyond Teff-ran's orbit, the fleet of fleeing Tefflans learned that Magya had yet one more weapon. A detector. Bombs. Bombs less than a half inch in diameter, bombs projected by the millions, from great momentum-wave guns, so that they traveled at a velocity of fifty miles a second—like the spreading pellets from a shot gun—bombs of luminous paint. They scattered in every direction in space. Meteors suddenly became luminescent. Ships, fleeing, lightless ships were suddenly visible—

With the joy bred of warfare, hatred incredibly old, the Magyan battleships threw themselves on their prey. The needle ships of Teff-el strove in vain to disintegrate the great machines. Their own walls, only inches in thickness, flashed in instantaneous incandescence, as two great transpon beams touched either end, and the shock of enormous, antigravity power coils poured through the framework.

They did not find some battleships. But they released nearly two thousand tiny one-man spy ships to dart about the space, and seek out every ship, every possible machine, and destroyers lingered behind to finish the job.

"This time," said Argan Matroh, Coördinator of Councils, "there shall not be even one ship to maintain that race." The battleships and the spy ships and the destroyers worked to that end.

But when hundreds of ships start out, all at one time, one, just one, might escape. There would be a careful search of every planet after this, just for certainty.

Aarn watched the screen ahead. There were other ships still on Teff-el, ships never designed to leave the planet, and incapable of it. They were scurrying back and forth madly. The ships were visible in the telescopic televisor.

"Orbital fort," said Spencer, pointing to a sudden, unfocused, black shadow that swam leisurely across the view. "Will they be dangerous?"

Aarn shrugged his shoulders. "Probably. They may be able to reach us with the new death-ray projectors. We will know sooner or later."

"Two hours and thirty-one minutes," said Spencer.

The planet was growing rapidly now. Far off to the left loomed Teff-ran, sweeping rapidly nearer. Teff-ran would not cross their path in this first circuit. "I hope they calculated the mass of those orbital forts right," sighed Aarn. "It will ruin our plans, if they don't give the right reaction."

"How?"

"We're supposed to hit three of them in this first swing, five in the next—if the thing works. We're going above orbital speed. Those collisions, with loss of momentum, or better, increase of mass, are counted on to slow us for an exceedingly elliptical orbit. The five, next time, will round out our orbit again, act as a resisting medium—molecules in a supergas to slow us down."

"I've been wondering—won't the shock of the tremendous mass of those forts be enough to split this moon wide open, split it, anyway, so that the momentum drive won't operate? Or so the apparatus here is smashed?"

———◦———

Aarn shook his head slowly. "They'll mainly bury themselves in this. We have fifty miles of solid rock above us. A fort—even one as huge as they are—will be of no great consequence. Remember, the rate of collision, the additive velocities, will make the relative velocities practically thirty-five miles a second. The result will be volatilization for the first fort, and for some of our rocky layer, the lower rate of collision of the second, will make it slightly less severe. The main thing, though, is that the rock won't transmit the shock at all!"

"Why not, it certainly isn't dough?"

"No, but—it can't transmit any shock, any push, at speed greater than the speed of sound through it. That speed of collision is greater than the speed of sound. Ergo, it won't be transmitted as a push. It will simply reduce the rock it hits to powder, expend its energy smashing the rock, breaking it, demolishing it—and not on moving."

"Also—why don't those orbital forts get out of the way?" asked Spencer.

"Combination of reasons. They could get part way out of the way at our present speed. That is, they could escape us once, but actually, this moon has greater mobility than they have. They were carried out by supply ships in pieces, and built up. They have motive power enough to turn around, and to straighten out their orbits so they won't tangle, but they can't flee. The main thing is that those Tefflans have courage. They will hope that the greater power of the forts may be able to do something against this moon, in the way of stopping it."

"Well, if their new beams will, won't they? If the battleships were dangerous—"

"The forts won't be. For two reasons. There are twenty-two forts, and only two battleships were equipped. You see that point?"

"They'd equip more battleships if they had time to manufacture the apparatus?"

"Yes—those were standard battleships—except for that feature. Anto Rayl says their investigators have found that those ships were two which had been for repairs at the time of the general debacle. They equipped those two, because a battleship can be more dangerous to this moon than a fort, even though a fort has greater power, since we could always reman the blamed thing, if they did kill us off, and the fort which killed us would be so much scrap buried in powdered rock.

"And the second point is—we've set up a heterodyne device that will tend to shift the frequency of those waves up to a higher, and harmless frequency. Harmless, because it is absorbed by their sound-conducting medium, the rock and steel. Provided they don't get too much power through. If they succeed in pounding it through even an absorbing medium, we'll be worse off, because the higher frequency is fatal more quickly."

"Pleasant thought. I wonder—" Twice a soft hum rose and fell musically.

"Carlisle," said Aarn, and flipped up the switch. Carlisle's image appeared slowly on the screen.

"Hello—hello—are you listening? I hope, since your Jupiter-dulled ears match your Jupiter-dulled wits, that you are. I'm about ten seconds away. You are sweeping in on line, and there is considerable anxiety among the forts. They've been trying to calculate your orbit, in at least two of them."

"How did you know that?" snapped Aarn, and went on listening.

"But haven't succeeded, since they can't allow for the effect of the collisions properly. Don't know your mass and all, nor how you will use your power, nor how great your power is. They think they'll be able to escape, most of 'em. They—eh—what? Oh—we learned easily enough. We smuggled some very useful investigators aboard. They haven't the new apparatus, by the way, and the Magyans here only mourn that they can't explore the whole fort. These darned things set up such a field, though, they are spotted the instant they move. The ones we're using now have been lying still now for nearly thirty-two hours. They came in along with the food supplies. We have some mighty ingenious and daring Magyans to thank for that. My idea of nerve. They made up three or four dozen crates of imitation food supply, and took them down a while ago, and planted them in Cantak, in a depot where a shipment of food for the forts was waiting. Made it and back without being spotted, thanks to the hubbub and general trouble down there, and now the investigators are loose on nearly all the forts." Carlisle paused for breath.

"That's what I call the long-distance, nonstop, polysyllabic, single-word speech," said Aarn, with a grin. "Fade off. I'm about to be busy. When you hear this, you'll know that merry voice of yours has been talking to a dead mike for twelve seconds." Aarn flipped his switch, and looked at the more-important scene ahead.

"They know which one we're headed for," he said, at length. The fort ahead was shifting, shifting distinctly from its cross-hair position. "I'll bet they strain a bed bolt pulling that crate, too."

The cross hairs were inclosed in a little circular target ring. The fort should have entered in that, about now, and they would be entering the range of the fort. Already their escort of powerful ships was falling away on every side, hastening away to leave the run-away moon to its work of attacking the fort.

Immediately a swarm of lesser Tefflan craft shot out from the direction of the fort, and came on directly in a line between fort and moon. Aarn smiled, and made some rapid adjustments.

"Destructive power on station thirty-four," he whispered tenderly into a microphone he picked up. Presently he pressed a button before him, reluctantly it seemed. Twin beams of transpon force reached out straight toward the fort, and Aarn manipulated them skillfully. A tremendous, blue-white arc flared at the far end, near the fort, and suddenly that arc was racing toward the Ma-ran. The transpon beams were opening apart like the legs of a divider, and an arc representing billions of horse power raced nearer Ma-ran.

Like moths in a flame, the bravely-attacking Tefflan ships exploded into nothing. The one-hundred-mile world, Ma-ran, loose and wandering to attack its foes, trundled solemnly, precisely toward the great fort, nearly five and a half miles in diameter, that loomed ahead.

Spencer, sitting near Aarn, had tuned in another, small television disk, and clearly now the picture inside the Tefflan fort was showing what the investigator within saw. Tefflans were scurrying around in wildest confusion.

"Send out all the torpedoes we have, and about half the heavy bombs. Turn the full power of the disintegrating ray on the surface where we will hit—" To the Tefflan it seemed the fort he was in was falling to the great surface, looming nearer and nearer. "Aggag Keenat, can we escape?"

"No, Master of Forts, there is no slightest possibility," said the astronomer calmly. "It matters little. They would move next to attack Teff-el. In this way, one of those missiles will be shattered, and if the prepared snare works—"

The fort was rapidly assuming the appearance of a disk now. And the torpedoes struck. Hundreds of them. They exploded and bored their way in through miles of rock. And yet not far enough to do damage. Then great bombs—the force of collision sank them half a mile, before they could ever explode. Then a great section of rock was blasted free.

"The trouble is," said Aarn judiciously, "that there is so little surface gravity here, that a good-sized ant could lift a boulder, and heave it out of the field of this vest-pocket planet."

"Even I admit this gravity is low," nodded Spencer. "Can you—ouch—that was a bad one—it jarred the whole moon."

"That," said Aarn, watching his screen carefully, "was the 'half the rest of the heavy bombs' he mentioned. They tore off—ah—that's better. They're falling back now." Aarn smiled contentedly. He had been working rapidly, and finally succeeded in getting his artificial gravity field which prevailed inside the planet, to spread outside. It was gripping those broken fragments now, and drawing them slowly back.

Aarn switched on a microphone before him. "Calling commander of fleets—commander of fleets—please give thought to my suggestion, and request, sir. The enemy is dropping powerful bombs in our path. The bombs break the rock, and will, if long continued, decrease the effectiveness of Ma-ran immeasurably. Suggest that you have a number of destroyers land on the forward side of Ma-ran, so close together that their various magnetic shields overlap, and thus protect the planet against the bombs."

The fort was scarcely a thousand miles away, as Aarn finished. Nearer and nearer it swept—nearer it expanded like a balloon—swept larger—

Fifteen seconds to go— "The first—it can't escape, Spence—ten—hold on!" The cry echoed through the speakers—five seconds— "She comes!"

The titanic mass of a hundred-mile sphere of rock and metal lumbered on—the mighty fort seemed poised, motionless. The flight of the fort was invisibly slow as they approached at thirty-two miles a second. It seemed the moon sprang at the fort, instantly reaching it, in those last few seconds. She seemed to accelerate with tremendous rapidity, decreasing the distance to zero in an instant—

A frightful burst of white-hot flame fanned out. A huge column of gas shot up, blazing white, searing flame heated beyond incandescence by the terrific impact, a gaseous column of steel vapor, thrown out by the electric flame of destroyed accumulators, bursting power plant—

The flame turned blue-green as the mercury flashed suddenly out in a momentary puff—

"The body has penetrated to a depth of ten and a quarter miles," announced a geologist assistant, coming up to Aarn.

"The next fort is now only one and three-quarter minutes away," snapped Aarn. "We've got to have that protective bunch of destroyers—ahhhhhhh listen—"

A continuous prolonged roar echoed and reëchoed through the rock. "The snare—I thought so—tons of explosives, and one ton would lift half the rock of this planet clear out of gravitative control without the artificial field until—"

"There is a hole, or completely broken spot in the rock twenty-two miles across, and a mile and a quarter deep," announced the assistant coming up.

"Uhmmm—not as bad as I feared. That isn't going to be a hole, because the artificial gravity field will draw it back. I think—we can let it go."

Again the signal rang out to hold on—again the sudden spread of a gigantic, expanding fort—and the terrible, soul-wrenching crash. The whole planet jarred slightly to it, and creaked.

"A crack has opened now, due to the close pits on the two forts. The commander of geological forces suggests you rotate the moon slowly—"

Another steel sphere was growing— Aarn saw that it was escaping them. "He had warning—we'd have hit him well on one side of our surface anyway—"

"We may graze him!"

"I doubt it—but I'll see." Rapidly Aarn's fingers flew over the control, and suddenly the great moon's structure creaked to a steady driving force, tremendous transpon beams flared and gleamed through the mighty cavern in its heart.

"He's going faster now!"

"So are we!" said Aarn grimly.

"We'll hit—no— Yes, by the planets—"

A terrible shrieking, grinding roar, a long-drawn howl of agony through the rocks—

And a fort like a dimpled, dented can rolled off clumsily, swiftly, end over end, and straight toward Teff-el!

"Broke his orbit!" cried Aarn. "He's ruined now, nothing can reform it for him."

"He's ruined anyway, the thing is past any effective work now."

"Don't you believe that, Spence! Those battleships are hard enough to stop, but every fort has sixteen separate power plants, and accumulators spread over the whole thing. There are some men always kept in acceleration-neutralizing apparatus—great spring chambers so arranged that no matter how the sudden acceleration might be applied, some would be sure to be saved. Two old battleship hulks were tied together once, and driven against one of the old forts, and killed off most of the crew. Never again, though. But that fort is done. It will be crushed on Teff-el."

CHAPTER XX

"THAT'S THE LAST FORT, Carlisle."

"I know it, Aarn. I'm aboard the *Sunbeam* now. Is your entrance still clear?"

"Perfectly. We saw to that. Where's the *Sunbeam*?"

"About ten thousand miles behind. Have you got that orbit checked?"

"Teff-ran is right in our swing—dead center—but they've got those hulks, you know—"

"What of it? They can't turn that, can they?"

"Somewhat. They'll slow it down, remember. Our velocity is only about ten miles a second—more than orbital speed, but they will mean something. What are they, exactly?"

"Every big freighter that could climb off Teff-el, loaded with rubbish, rock, scrap steel, ingots, everything heavy they could cram into them. They're still adding to it. Won't it break up the moon? And will they slow you down so much—"

"Whoa—wait. They'll slow us down, but they won't interfere with the plan. Remember, this is our fourth circling. We've acquired the added mass of all those forts. We're distinctly heavier now, so heavy we can scarcely maneuver with the driving equipment we have. Those ships will be swept into us, and add to the mass. We'll lose velocity—but we won't lose momentum. The momentum will be the same, we can leave, and the moon will smash Teff-ran with just enough momentum to stop it dead, if the figures we have are right. Then she'll drop on Teff-el."

"Couldn't you dodge that bunch of ships, and get more momentum and velocity so you'd hit Teff-el harder?"

"Ha—vindictive, aren't you? Why knock a planet when it's down-ey powder. The thing will be ruined anyway!"

"All right. What do I do?"

"Slip in that opening. You have your guard?"

"Three battleships."

"All right—slip in. There are only five of us left. We'll be all ready to get into the *Sunbeam*, and leave here just about ten seconds before the smash. They've rigged an outside jury control. We'll operate that. I'm putting on a space suit."

"Check—do I come now?"

"Right." Aarn cut the switch, and attended strictly to business. "Got that final detonator rigged, Spence?"

"Right. Are we going to leave before Ma-ran hits those ships or after?"

"Before—they aren't like the forts. These are concentrated mass. Remember, the forts were ninety per cent open rooms. Those cargo boats have been stuffed with everything heavy they could find, and then loaded further when they were in place out there. They'll go through so far they may actually reach down here."

"Hmmmmm—they may. Everything rigged on your end?"

"Everything. And the *Sunbeam's* in the outer lock already. Ten miles a second—check exactly. Leave the autos in control, I guess—till we get above." Aarn rapidly set the controls to respond as he wished and in a moment they were whirling up in the *Sunbeam*.

Up through the long tunnel, still glowing with the lights. Nearly all the energy was drained from the great coils now, and a great deal of the most valuable apparatus had been salvaged, the instruments in particular. Still, one bank of coils contained its full energy potential, enough to run the mighty engine for about ten minutes on full power. Aarn had started that, and the Ma-ran was accelerating now.

The *Sunbeam* rose with some difficulty, the two systems of momentum waves fighting each other in a slight blue, wavering luminescence about the ship. "She's drawing a lot of power," Spencer remarked.

In seconds the ship was out of the tunnel, propelled at the last by a blast of escaping air. Ma-ran was airless now. Swiftly the ship raced around the little world, around the incredibly tortured forward side. Immense craters dotted the surface, huge holes, and mighty piles of tumbled rock. They landed, and examined the broken stone. Aarn laughed, and picked up one nearly ten feet square, and threw it a quarter of a mile, as he walked toward the little heap of instruments and apparatus glistening in the sunlight. Swiftly he fastened several heavy cables to the *Sunbeam*, then looked at his instruments. The chronometer, the registering velocispectrometer, and the momentumometer were most important.

Then he looked up. Directly overhead floated a maze of dancing, moving points of light, which were slowly, steadily spreading and separating, widening across his sky. And beyond, the disk of Teff-ran, to one side of the greater, shining crescent of Teff-el. A swarm of great battleships seemed to be sliding steadily about Ma-ran, and beyond them a greater swarm of smaller ships. Aarn carefully aligned the huge missile he was launching, checked his coördinates carefully, and finally cut off the acceleration he had been using.

Then he pushed a button. Quickly now, he pulled a heavy, double-handed, swordlike ax from its resting place, swung it above his head, and brought it down with all his power on the heavy-armored cables that, wired together, twisted off across the incredible jumble of rocks to the shaft that plunged fifty miles to the center of Ma-ran, and severed it. Instantly, then, he leaped for the entrance of the *Sunbeam* with the instrument panel in his arms. The ship started up as he reached it, the controls he had lately been using dangling on the steel cable as the ship darted swiftly up and away.

Scarcely had he left the surface when something began to happen. From the mouth of the great tunnel, gases were still pouring, but now they were suddenly tinged with red, and then greenish white, and they plunged out in an explosive flame.

As the *Sunbeam* swept up, the view Aarn had was, for the first time, as an outsider. The majesty of the scene came to him suddenly—the great dark sphere, rugged and cold in the sunlight, the dust motes of the Tefflan freighters daring to oppose it, and, further away, the great mass of Teff-ran.

And now, away from the moon, he saw at last Ma-kanee. Deserted, uncontrolled, and uncontrollable, she was plunging straight for Teff-el. And Teff-el was already drawing her. Seas on Teff-el were rising, tides appearing, for already the swift-moving moon was within 1,000,000 miles of the planet. There had been no attempts to divert it. That was frankly impossible. Further attempts to escape from Teff-el had been made, but there was a great ring now, of far-flung spy ships, each with a tremendous magnetic atmosphere thrown out, and the first touch of a ship attempting to escape made itself very evident. And the fields overlapped.

—◇—

Minutes passed swiftly. And now the mass of Tefflan ships ahead, deserted, had separated to individuals. Minutes more passed, and at last the terrific process that had been going on within Ma-ran became evident. A dull glow began to appear in the rocks below. It was growing swiftly—

The first great Tefflan freighter plowed into Ma-ran. It was swallowed up like a pebble sinking into water—and with the same splashing of liquid. Almost instantly, a tremendous fountain of white-hot lava snapped out—and impaled a second freighter that was almost in line with the first. Both tumbled to the mad moon. A dozen were falling—a hundred—

In seconds Ma-ran was sweeping on through a clear space. Every one of the great Tefflan ships had been absorbed. One of them had barely grazed the world, but been caught, and lay a pool of lighter, molten stuff on the rock pool. Great hot bubbles of air were oozing slowly up from the ships.

"Velocity fell only one point. That was good enough. We reach Teff-ran now in three quarters of an hour," said Aarn at last.

The minutes dragged. The two great bodies seemed to move with infinite weary slowness. They seemed to know doom was upon them, and were going to it with the slow steadiness of men who welcomed doom, but accepted it philosophically and without hurry.

Further and further the *Sunbeam* and her escort drew away, now. She raced ahead to a position in line with the final meeting, and watched as the two great balls of matter moved leisurely toward each other.

Ma-ran looked like an orange drifting gently toward a grapefruit. Ma-ran was at last the smaller as she approached the end of her mad career. And beyond the great crescent of Teff-el, and the approaching disk of Ma-kanee, Tefflan ships swarmed up from Teff-ran—and a swarm of heavy Magyan cruisers fell on them instantly, and cut them to pieces.

Ma-ran bulged slowly, seemed to lengthen, and hastened her wild pace as she neared Teff-ran. Glowing red with the liberated energy of her coils, she stretched, became a blunt-ended cylinder—and slowly became two great balls of red-hot matter as she began to turn visibly.

"Gyroscopes went—the impact of the ships—" muttered Aarn uneasily. "That may have some unlooked-for effect—"

Soundlessly, softly, with a sudden increased blaze of light, the two masses met, and spattered. Ma-ran coalesced with Teff-ran, and stopped. Teff-ran split. Slowly, majestically, they saw chasms open and run about the world. The sides fell away, and kept on going. The second half of Ma-ran struck, and spread like a drop of melted lead on a hard surface—and the slipping sides of Teff-ran were snared, and melted in the flaming blue-white heat of the collision. In a quarter of an hour both bodies were one, and the mass was white-hot, flames spurting out angrily.

Hours passed, as Aarn hung grimly beside the glowing mass. Finally he was satisfied with his observations, and made his calculations. "Six hours. Ma-kanee will get there in about six hours, two minutes and thirty seconds. This will get there at almost the same time. My calculations aren't quite accurate. I can't allow for the displacement of Teff-el for one thing."

The new mass was dropping. Slowly—steadily. Wildly, small ships were shooting up from Teff-el, vindictively heading toward a cruiser or battleship with all its power, hoping to smash through the great wall even as a pilot died. They flamed briefly in a great transpon beam, and died—unsuccessful.

Ma-kanee moved steadily downward. Tefflans were out on the surface of the planet, black masses of them, moving and surging, as they watched the two great bodies falling out of the skies on two exactly opposite sides.

Three hours. Four hours. Five hours. The heat of the new mass, glowing red, had driven the black masses to other parts of the world. Cracks were appearing in Teff-el now. The new mass was only slightly distorted.

"Teff-el's gravitational field declines slowly in strength—mass is so great—doesn't pull the near side much harder than the far side, so they don't fall apart, as Ma-ran did."

But Teff-el began to fall apart. Great cracks appeared, smoke began to curl up, and over the great cavern system of Cantak, the ground sank suddenly, and an abrupt fault line appeared that sectioned the city with the precision of a knife. And slowly Teff-el turned under the baleful glare of the new, red-hot menace.

Five hours and a half. The red-hot mass was nearing the outer fringes of the atmosphere. It was falling swiftly, now, still circling the planet a bit, so that its contact would not be a center blow, but a gouging scrape. An entire fleet of battleships was pulling at it now with traction beams, but there was practically no effect. The mass was too great, the beams almost totally useless.

At the end of six hours, Ma-kanee entered the atmosphere. The atmosphere instantly compressed under it, a great bubble of air, and simultaneously, for the three seconds it took the planet to traverse the atmosphere, everything beneath that place was compressed under a stupendous air pressure. It mounted like a solid wave; the air could not move away in time—

Ma-ran-teff-ran struck the other side. The atmosphere flamed below, and the planet caught fire from the terrible, glowing coal. Almost simultaneously, with a precision that was astounding, two bodies struck Teff-el.

And the planet burst like a rotten tomato. Spurts of liquid stuff shot suddenly out of mighty chasms. Bursts that were cold, and solidified instantaneously into weird shafts of solid, grainless, incredible rock. Jets of rock, then great sections of rock, then a great jet of flying, gleaming metal, that squirted out like water from a hose, and solidified as the rock had, and in a bar ten miles through and a hundred and fifty long.

And then only parts, and broken splinters that began to stop flying apart, remained. They were glowing, and some of them struck, and stuck together, and the force of their striking made them glow more, and cemented them.

All three bodies were utterly destroyed, but the heat of Ma-ran-teff-ran remained, and seemed to act as a binding agent.

"Well—the ancient enemy is gone. Destroyed after some forty thousand years of trying."

"And Teff-el is destroyed."

"But while Tefflans can never reform, Teff-el is already reforming. See how the parts are falling together. It will be centuries, milleniums, before it is a planet again. But Teff-el is not destroyed. An incident in its life has taken place." Aarn gazed at the planet's disintegrating parts.

EPILOGUE

"The apparatus is installed, Anto Rayl, the problem has been solved, and we have left apparatus with you. We must go now. Our home is on the other side of the wall, but we can both climb that wall now—so we of Earth will expect to see you of Magya soon. Will you come?"

"Certainly we will come, Aarn Munro. We will want to see the Ancient World, where men such as those we have met are bred, and where the race was born.

"We do not like to see you go. We wish you could stay, but we realize your situation. We will attempt to follow you through at the end of one thousand days.

"So—till then." Anto Rayl, standing in the airlock of the *Sunbeam* waved, turned, and dived across space to the entrance port of a great gleaming metal wall, a mighty battleship wall.

"They won't need those any more," said Aarn thoughtfully, and set up his controls.

Anto Rayl looked back—and saw suddenly that the *Spencer Research Laboratories Number Six* was going. Going off with infinite speed into infinite distance, or into infinite smallness. He couldn't tell which—

www.ingramcontent.com/pod-product-compliance
Lightning Source LLC
Chambersburg PA
CBHW011446170626
46816CB00008B/2550